I0591123

KILLIAN

THE O'FARRELL BROTHERS

BOOK 2

KATE BONHAM

ISBN (Print): 978-0-6456537-7-9

Cover Design by Wingfield Designs

Editing by Ravenna Poe Edits

MIDNIGHT DREARY
PUBLISHING

PLAYLIST

It Ain't Over 'Til It's Over - Lenny Kravitz

Million Reasons - Lady Gaga

Nothing Breaks Like a Heart - Mark Ronson & Miley Cyrus

The Unforgiven - Metallica

Until I Found You - Stephen Sanchez

Say Something - A Great Big World & Christina Aguilera

PROLOGUE

KILLIAN

The tears in her eyes told me it wasn't going to go my way today. I'd noticed her pulling away for weeks now. The more I got involved with my father's business, the more she became silent. She wasn't built for this world.

She wasn't on board with the criminal aspect that came with being part of the O'Farrell family. I had no choice but she did.

"Sloane..."

"Killian, I...I can't be this woman. I'm not strong like your mum."

"Babe," I tried to pull her to me but she pulled away, her arm twisting out of my grip. The simple loss of her skin on mine made my chest pull in a weird way. We'd been together for two years. We may only be eighteen but I had known from the day I met her that I'd wanted to marry her. She was too kind for this world.

Too beautiful, too lovely.

She deserved more.

"I understand," I said, my voice breaking with emotion. "You have to do what you need to do."

"Don't be like that," she said, coming into my arms. I rested my hands on her hips, loving how they fit perfectly over her. She'd always felt so comforted by them being there. It sucked this would probably be the last time I could feel her this way.

"What way should I be, Sloane?" I asked her. "You're breaking my fucking heart here."

She laid her lips on mine, tears running down her beautiful cheeks. I pushed harder against her mouth, tasting her tongue on mine. I moaned into her mouth, my hand twisting in her hair as our kissing became more intense. My cock was pushing against my jeans, hard, wanting to be freed and to be inside of her immediately.

I knew that wasn't going to happen.

This was goodbye. I could feel it. I pulled back on my own tears and made sure she knew what she was giving up. Sloane wrapped her arms around my neck as I pulled her down into the backset of the car. She straddled my legs as she devoured my mouth with hers.

Until she stopped.

Sloane rested her head against mine, our breaths heavy and mingled. She pushed up off me, and got out of the car, turning her back to me. She put one hand on her waist and looked out at the sea below. I willed my cock to calm the fuck down before I pulled out of the car and slammed the back door shut out of frustration. I opened the car door and got in behind the wheel before I slammed the door shut.

Sloane turned around, her eyes were red and full of tears as she moved closer to the car but she made no attempt to get in.

"Can you really see me being your wife someday, Kill?"

"You know what?" I spat back at her as I turned the ignition. "I did."

I sped off, leaving her standing on top of the cliff, too angry to return for her. She knew her way home from there. It was the cruelest thing I could think to do to her that wouldn't break my heart even more than it already was.

She'd destroyed me.

She didn't want to fight for me like I would for her.

I sped toward the estate, our family home, and parked in the usual spot. Stomping up the stairs, I quickly avoided my brothers and my father and slammed my door shut. The tears poured freely now, as I looked at the bag I'd packed earlier today. The note I'd written to say my goodbyes to the family still sat on the dresser, unread.

I'd chosen Sloane.

I had chosen to leave Ireland to be with her by skipping out on being an O'Farrell...for her.

But she'd not given me the chance to tell her.

She'd made up her mind.

And I had to accept that.

I put my clothes away and tossed my empty bag into the bottom of my cupboard. Grabbing the note, I pulled a lighter from my back pocket out and I lit the corner of the note, watching it burn. I tossed it into my bin as I saw the flames climb, erasing my letter and my intentions.

I was an O'Farrell and for the rest of my life, I'd never love again.

CHAPTER ONE

KILLIAN

FIFTEEN YEARS LATER

The mundane thumping of the DJ's insipid music was drilling through my head as the club pumped. I could think of nothing worse than this drivel they pumped through the club with no lyrics or the same lyrics played over and over and calling it a song but it was popular with the young ones that came here on weeknights and kept my club from falling in the red. I checked my phone again but I hadn't heard from the one person I'd wanted to hear from. Message after message from women all around town wanting me to end the night in their bed.

But I only wanted one.

Since Sloane had found her way back into my life through her best friend Teeghan, I couldn't get her off my mind. It was messing with my stamina, and my libido. I got off the chair and leaned on the railing, looking down at the party below. I should be happy my club was doing so well, but it did mean I was here most nights, making sure no one tried anything. After the shoot out at this place months ago, I had been trying desperately to show that this place was a safe haven. I'd tightened security and had more cameras added. Slowly, the people came back. It had only been a matter of time anyway, this was the only club in town worth going to.

I was about to make my way back to my office when I saw a woman sitting at the bar, sipping at her drink. I hadn't seen her in months and was more than a little surprised she was back here. I made my way down the stairs, pushing through the throng of people to get to the bar. Sidling up to her, I motioned for the bartender to slide a drink my way.

"Amity."

She turned to look at me, those piercing blue eyes looking straight through me. The last time I'd seen her, she had been crying into my shirt over her dead husband. Whereas hours before I'd given her the grim news, she'd been bouncing up and down on my cock behind his back. Now, it looked like she wanted to murder me.

"Killian."

"You haven't been around lately. What brings you by tonight?" I asked her as I sipped at my bourbon.

"I have to have a reason to visit a club?" she asked me as she downed the rest of her cocktail.

"You've never been one to come here," I responded. "You always told me you'd never come here just to see my tight ass."

She smirked, but it held no humor behind it. Rather, it felt like she had ice running through her veins. It was clear she was still grieving.

"Perhaps I came here to tell you something," she said, swiveling around to face me. Her dress was low cut, a deep v showed that ample cleavage I knew she had, and the split went all the way up to her pantyline. She came here with a purpose.

I just knew I wasn't going to like it though.

"And that is?"

She slid off the bar stool and leaned in close. Close enough I could smell her expensive Chanel perfume.

"I've come back for revenge," she said in my ear. "And first up is your little brother Conor. He's the one who killed my husband. He's in love now, isn't he?"

She bit my earlobe and drew her teeth across it before she winked at me and walked away. I was too stunned to move.

A threat on the family is a threat on all of us.

She'd just fired her first shot and now I had to protect my little brother.

Again.

God fucking damn it.

I downed the rest of my drink and moved out of the club and toward the back door. I pulled my phone out and dialed Lorcan.

"What?" he responded, half asleep. I checked my clock and saw it read it was just past 1 in the morning.

Fuck.

"We got a huge fucking problem. I'm coming to the estate."

"Do you need Conor?" he asked, already sounding more alert than he did two seconds ago.

"No, leave him. We'll bring him in soon enough."

Lorcan hung up and I sped my way to the estate. Conor had finally gotten his happy ever after, I wasn't going to let a bereaved woman spoil that for him. Not with everything those two have already been through.

———

LORCAN WAS ALREADY at the table when I arrived. I sat down next to him and put my phone face down to save on distractions. I already knew how Lorcan was going to react, with a stern face rub and a pinch on the bridge of his nose.

"What's so urgent?" Lorcan asked me.

"I bumped into Amity at the club."

"And?"

He was unconcerned because he knew of our past, but I could already feel the tension rising in this room.

"And she may or may not have subtly warned me she's going to get her revenge on our little brother."

Lorcan rubbed his hand over his face just like our father did when he was dealt troubling news. Our father had never had to worry about his brothers like we did. I thought I'd always be the troublesome middle child but turns out our baby bro was getting a reputation enough for all of us.

"How serious do you think she is?"

The memory of her biting my earlobe and whispering the threat was enough to make me want to wince. "I'd say she's serious."

"Do you think she'd have the contacts to pull off whatever she's planning?"

"Lor, she disappeared after his death. No one had seen her for months, and now she turns up and has a stare that could slice you in two."

"Got it," he said. "Call in the boys, have her followed."

I nodded. "What do you want to tell Conor?"

"You were right not to tell him yet," Lorcan said. "Let's see if we can contain this threat before it lands at his feet. He and Teeghan deserve a little bit of peace."

I nodded. Lorcan and Teeghan had become best friends since she and Conor had become a thing. I'd never seen Lorcan trust anyone without the O'Farrell name but she somehow had him opening up about the wounds of his past. I was glad for it. The man needed to stop acting like a wounded soldier and get himself some puss. Maybe then, he wouldn't always be such a grouch.

I didn't mind Teeghan either. She had a killer sense of humor and she loved to play pranks on Conor. It was hilarious to watch as he slowly lost his shit only to realize it hadn't been one of us, but his woman instead.

Teeghan was all right in my books, and being best friends with Sloane meant she was an asset to the family if only to keep Sloane in my periphery.

I stood up, and grabbed my phone. "I'll head out to gather the boys."

"Do you know where she's living?"

"I assume it's at her old house but I can go by and check it out. It's on the way to my apartment."

Lorcan nodded and went back to whatever the fuck he'd been doing before I came here. I made a quick exit and got in my car.

That was painless, I only prayed Amity wasn't going to be a real concern and this was all to get me up in a flap. I didn't want the woman to be killed.

She'd endured enough.

Putting my car into gear, I tore out of the long driveway and headed into town, toward my place with way too many things on my mind for a Tuesday night.

SLOANE

THE SEA AIR was refreshing even with this cloudy weather we'd been having. There was just something about being by the sea that made everything become more clear. I had come down here to get away but now all I wanted to do was clear it out so I could sell it.

This has been the home Sean and I had wanted to settle into with a family. I couldn't do that anymore, and there was no reason to keep it. That dream had died the day he perished.

I wrapped my shawl around me tighter as I sipped at my coffee, with a dash of irish whiskey to wake me up. The waves crashed against the rocks around the shore, and the wind howled around me. Being away from everyone else had been refreshing but it was long past due that I join the living again. I was so close to being done going through all the things Sean had left here, and now I only had some boxes I had been storing here to go through. Memories had been tearing me apart for weeks now, and I'd been doing it alone. Teeghan had been checking in, sure, but I didn't want her to be pulled down into my misery. She was in a new relationship and she was enjoying the perks that came with that, such as mind blowing sex. I couldn't even remember the last time I'd had sex. Surely, it had been with Sean but I couldn't tell you how long it had been before his tragic accident.

Fuck.

I needed to get back to living. This was depressing me in more ways than I could fathom. I needed to see Teeghan. She grounded me in ways that I didn't realize I needed.

I finished my coffee and went back inside, undoing my shawl and tossing it on the couch filled with boxed up memories.

As I opened the top of the box of my past, I looked

down at the familiar notebooks and most notably my diary. It was my high school diary. I chuckled out loud even though no one would hear it as I picked it up and started to flip through the pages of childish writing, where I had dotted my i's with big love hearts. That had been when I'd been in love.

Images of Killian filled my memory as I came to a page in the diary with something on it. The necklace dropped down at my feet as I looked down at it and felt a big lump form in my throat. I remember the day he gave this to me.

Bending down, I picked up the necklace and ran my finger over the fine engravings on the cross. It was his family crest on a cross. An heirloom of their family's and he had given it to me. I couldn't believe I still had it.

We'd not been together for fifteen years.

I looked down at the page I had kept it in and saw the love hearts adorning the page and I read the words that broke my heart all over again.

"Today, I ended it with Killian. My heart is breaking into a million pieces and I just don't know what to do about it. It's for the best, I know this, but it's killing me. The way he looked at me, the way he took it and didn't fight for me. It burns me inside but I know...I just know it's the only way forward. He's too dark for me. He wants to be like his da, and I don't want to end up like his mother. I kept his necklace. I can't part with it yet. Is that wrong?"

I closed the diary and put it back in the box and looked back down at the necklace. I pulled my phone from my back pocket and looked through my contacts.

His number was under Z Killian, so he didn't come up until the end of my contacts. It was to stop myself from calling him when I was feeling low. There had been so many times since he'd come back into my life these past few months that I had wanted to see or speak to him. Every time I did see him, my whole world would turn upside down for days. I'd dream about the things I wanted him to do to me, I'd smile at memories of our happier days, and then I would drift into a miserable depression until I could pull myself out.

He was my weakness, he always had been. I loved my husband. I had loved every bit of him and still did, but Killian...there was just something about him I could never stop loving. I didn't think you could love more than one person at the same time, but I'd proven that you could. Sean had been dead for years now but I still held guilt over never being able to say I no longer loved Killian.

I sat down on the one bit of my lounge and opened the contact I rarely used. Typing a message, I hovered my finger over the send button for a few seconds before I hit it and felt my stomach cave in on itself.

Why did I invite him here?

I should have just gone back to the city and given it back to him there, where I had witnesses, where I wouldn't be tempted to invite him in and have his cologne invade my senses.

———

I HEARD his car pull up outside and my heart did a flutter before my stomach decided to burn whatever acid it had in there. Why did I suddenly need to use the bathroom?

Getting off the couch, I rubbed my sweaty hands down my jeans and took a deep breath. I checked my reflection in the mirror on the wall just as I heard his heavy knock on my door.

I felt like I was sixteen again and he had come to pick

me up for the first date, although, to be honest, I had run to the door then to take him outside before my father could pull me back inside and slam the door in his face.

I finally reached the door and opened it. His cologne wafted in and I felt myself transported back to my childhood when I used to love his cologne, even though he used far too much of it back then. Killian's cocky smirk appeared on his face as he looked at me.

"Hey."

"Come in, Killian."

He moved past me, and I could almost taste the leather as he moved into the cottage. I never realized before just how small this place was, especially with Killian in it.

"You're moving?"

"I am going to sell it, yes."

He turned to face me, confusion etched onto his face. "But this was your dream."

"No, it was my dream with Sean."

He sobered at the mention of his name. He may not have liked that I had moved on, but he never once made life hard for Sean, even though he could have. He'd learned that I was happy and he made sure to steer clear of us.

Not that it mattered.

My heart already held a piece of Killian in it, forever.

"Why did you want me to come?" he asked, finally.

I pulled the necklace from my jeans pocket and held it out to him. "I found this in an old diary. I thought you should get it back, I've held it hostage long enough."

He looked down at the necklace, and took it from my hand. I hadn't realized how heavy it had been once I was holding it. When he took the weight of it off me, I felt suddenly empty.

A feeling I hadn't felt for years now.

He smiled as he traced over the cross and its fine engraving. "I can't believe you still had this."

"I'm a packrat, as you can see. I never throw anything away, especially old school diaries."

He finally looked back up at me, a look in his eye that I couldn't read. He stepped closer to me, and suddenly I felt myself suck in a deep breath. He grabbed my hand and put the necklace back in it, closing my fingers over it.

"You should keep it. I have no need for it."

His close proximity was enough for my brain to leave the building and my heart to start commanding me to do things I really shouldn't. I looked up into his eyes, and I saw the same dark eyes that I remembered from when we were kids.

When I knew he wanted me just as I wanted him.

I felt my teeth drag my bottom lip in just as the blood rushed down to my pussy, and instantly I felt the familiar throb that I knew would cause me to do something I knew I'd regret.

His hand was on mine, still and I felt the heat from it on mine.

Within mere moments, and before I could react, his other hand was on the side of my face and his lips crashed down on mine. He walked me backward until I felt the wall against my back. His tongue tangled with mine in a heated ferocity that had my pussy throbbing, my legs becoming weak.

I'd never wanted him like I knew I needed him right now. His body crushed against mine, molding into all the right spots, just like it did back in the day.

God.

Was this happening?

Maybe just one more time with him. One more bout in the sack and I'd be free of him.

Surely.

I think I already knew that wasn't the case, and this was going to complicate things further, but I couldn't stop it.

Not now.

He groaned into my mouth and I knew this was going to happen. I was never going to be able to pull away from him.

The universe was willing this to happen.

His rough fingers went up under my shirt, the callused ridges of his fingers caused a slight friction on my skin that went directly down my nerves and straight to my pussy. I moaned into his mouth which caused him to lift me up on the wall, placing his leg between my legs to hold me in place.

With what seemed like the universe righting itself, his phone rang.

Instantly, I pulled away from his mouth and he grunted. I didn't know if it was in pain or if it was in annoyance.

He gently put me back down on my feet. I quickly reached out to make sure I didn't fall down. My legs were not sturdy right now. Killian pulled his phone out and answered it with a growl.

"What?"

Another throb after hearing him growl into the phone. I wanted that growl in my ear, as he did things to me down south with those delicious fingers.

He listened for a moment, and I realized just how close I came to desecrating this cottage I shared with Sean by being with Killian.

I took a deep breath and tried to compose myself.

"Fine. I'll be there."

He hung up and looked back over at me. I could feel his

intense gaze on me for a few moments before that cocky smirk made its way back on his face and he headed for the door. I realized the necklace was still in my hand, draped over several fingers.

"But you gave this to me when you thought we'd be endgame. Isn't this for who you think you'll marry?"

I knew Lorcan and Conor had been given one too from their father, and I remember seeing their mother wearing one.

"We are endgame, Sloane."

He left the cottage, and me reeling. Once his car tore out of my driveway and away, I suddenly felt like I could breathe again as I sat down on the couch and willed my pussy to go back into a dormant stance.

Fucking Killian O'Farrell.

KILLIAN

I PULLED into the parking lot of the warehouse and got out, making sure my gun was loaded. My man Omar was in charge of this part of my business, and he was usually unstoppable but lately, he was having issues with a new drug running power popping up in England who thinks they run Ireland too. I'd taken out every single one of them they sent over here to scope us out, but it seemed they had a bigger operation than we did. Opening the back door, I headed inside to see the operation going smoothly. The marajuana and cocaine divisions of my business were working well. I refused to deal in meth, but I knew I was going to have to do it eventually. My ecstasy operation was at a different warehouse.

"O."

Omar turned around, relieved.

"I locked them up in the back room."

I nodded and headed inside, Omar by my side for the backup I knew I wouldn't need. As I kicked open the door, I saw the two men, their hands tied behind their back all but shit themselves, one even fell off his chair and landed with a thud on the cement floor.

I held back the laugh as I closed the door behind us and made sure they saw my gun before I stood against the wall. The single lightbulb in the room was swinging from side to side casting an eerie glow over the room.

"Get up," Omar growled as he pulled the guy up and put him back on the chair as hard as possible.

"Who sent you here?" I asked them, calmly.

Silence.

Omar circled them like a shark, and I could see the fear written all over their faces, even though they tried to hide it.

"I won't ask again."

"No one sent us," one of them quivered. "We came alone."

"I don't quite believe that," I replied. "Now, come on, don't make me torture you before I kill you."

They shared a look and I could see some kind of shield coming down between them. Omar continued his stalking, getting closer and closer with every circle he made around them. The pressure was mounting for them to tell me, and they knew it. There was no way I could let them live after the disrespect they had caused my family.

"Lukas Porter."

"What was that?" I asked, pushing off the side wall and coming closer.

"Lukas Porter," he said with a firm voice. "He is who sent us here."

"Shut your hole, Peter."

I turned my attention to the one who had fallen off his chair and was now staring daggers at the loose lipped one. Pulling out my gun, I shot at the one who was trying to silence Peter, blood trickling from his head wound.

Peter looked at me now, his fear showing.

"Tell me about Lukas."

I kneeled in front of him and he whimpered, his lip shaking with the motion.

"He runs all of London."

"And?"

"And what?" Peter spat, angry. I usually saw this emotion when they knew they would die. They expended all of their energy into anger because you were about to take their life.

"What else do I need to know?" I asked him.

"We aren't the only ones."

"Tell me what you know."

"Why," he groaned in pain. I saw the gaping wound on his leg as he tried not to move. "You're just going to kill me."

"Who knows," I replied quickly. "I may take pity on the wounded. Tell me everything and I'll see what I can do for you."

Omar grinned behind him. He knew what my mercy could do for people. Omar, himself, was someone I granted mercy to a long time ago. His loyalty knew no bounds and I trusted him as much as I did my own brothers now.

"Lukas means to take Ireland just like he did with Scotland and England."

"What?" I replied. "He took Scotland?"

Peter nodded. "Yes. Recently. Now he wants Ireland."

Fucker.

"What happened to Callum?"

Callum had been a strong opponent. Someone I would want on my team but I knew he'd never leave his post in Scotland. If Lukas had defeated him, we would have had a serious problem on our hands.

"He joined him."

My worst fears were realized in just three words. I backed up, back to the wall where I had been before.

"Where do I find him?"

"He finds you," Peter said just as Omar slid the rope around his neck and began to strangle him to death. Peter struggled against it, trying to claim some kind of power over his life but after a few minutes, he was lifeless. Omar released the rope and Peter's body dropped to the floor with a thud.

I felt nothing for the lifeless form of the man who had come here to fuck up my life. Only now, I knew he had been successful. He was a nobody and he had rattled me.

Callum had been bought.

Callum fucking Mackenzie had given in to a new power. There was only one reason he would do that.

Lukas Porter was someone to be feared.

Omar sighed heavily as he headed over to me. "I'll clean this up and call you once it's all done."

I nodded quickly and exited the room, wanting to scream but I didn't want to show my employees I was worried. I quickly found my way to my car and headed to the gym. It was the only place I could go and get my head right by punching with someone or by using the beat up old bag that could crush your knuckles if you didn't know how to use it.

I parked in the no parking zone out the front and headed in. The smell of sweat and stale air hit my senses immediately. I could see some of Ireland's biggest boxers in the ring, having a match, as others watched on, wanting to be them some day. Most of Ireland's legendary boxers came through this gym on their way to glory and they always came back to inspire the younger generation.

It was the family feel of the place.

I'd thought I would channel my rage through boxing for Sloane. I would escape the dungeon that was my family and become a famous boxer, giving her the life she deserved, but I'd been pulled in the wrong direction and couldn't get out.

It only got worse after Dad died.

"Killian."

I spun around to see Neil, the gym owner and one of the best boxing trainers that ever lived, coming over to me.

"Hey, champ."

He'd also been a boxing champ in local shows but had never quite made it to the big show. I knew it had something to do with the fact his wife and daughter had been killed by the IRA back in the day. It had kept him local, urging the youth of the day to steer clear of the IRA and keep their noses clean. For the most part, they did.

"Been a while since I saw your ugly mug in here."

I smirked at him as I turned back to the boxing match in the ring. I knew the boxer parading around like a peacock in front of me.

We'd been in school together and he'd always been a ponce.

"When did Brendan Kelly get back in town?"

"He comes back every year to visit his family," Neil told me. "He's not such a dickhead as he was back then. You should give him a chance."

"Never," I replied. "That fuckhead is lucky to be walking and breathing now."

I remembered what the asshole had done to my brother

when he'd been all of twelve. Conor hadn't been the same for almost two years after.

"Give him a chance, Killian."

I'd never wanted to punch someone in the face as much as I did right now and after my little run in with the boys from London, I wanted to do it even more.

Only with a gun.

"You need to blow off some steam?" Neil asked.

I nodded.

"Come on."

I headed back with him. He grabbed the tape and began to tape my hands. We were silent and he left the room once he was done. I pulled my jacket and shirt off, leaving the singlet I had on underneath. I grabbed a water bottle from the side of the room and filled it with water before I headed out to the bags.

Brendan had a captive audience around him as I shrugged off the hatred I had for the man and the memory of seeing my little brother beaten and bloody that fateful day. The fucker deserved to be in prison or six feet under, and I'd held back.

I'll forever regret that decision.

As I got into the mindset of bashing the bag in front of me, I removed Brendan, and thought of the stressors from the London invasion and how the hell I was going to get Sloane out of my mind.

Hell, I knew how ridiculous that was. She'd never left my mind since the day I met her.

I knew she'd always be a part of me, whether she was with me or not.

"Shit, is that you Killian O'Farrell?"

I gritted my teeth as I turned to face Brendan Kelly and hopefully not act on my impulses and end up in prison.

CHAPTER TWO

KILLIAN

EIGHTEEN YEARS EARILER

I winced once my sunglasses were removed from my eyes. The day was bright, and sunny. A rare occurrence, but they certainly did happen.

"You're going to go to all your classes," Lorcan said, angrily. "And you're going to pay attention and fucking graduate in two years. Understand?"

I put my fingers up to my eyebrow and saluted him. The alcohol from last night made my stability a little shady as I laughed on my way down to my ass.

"Get your fucking ass up, boy," Lorcan all but ground out. "Don't have me call father."

That sobered me up quickly. I grabbed my sunglasses off him again and stumbled my way down the pathway to the school grounds. My bag was slipping off my shoulder as I headed into the front courtyard of the school. The school administrator was close to coming over and telling me to get out before I saw the most beautiful girl stand in front of me and guide me toward the side entrance, away from the administrator. She acted like we were laughing as she took most of my weight to make it look like I was steady on my feet.

Once we were away from the witch of an administrator, the girl put me down on a bench. She sat down next to me, and her sweet perfume drifted into my nostrils.

"I'm Sloane."

I looked into her pretty eyes and felt as if my insides were melting. Maybe it was just the alcohol, but something inside told me it was her.

"Killian."

"Nice to meet you. We just moved back here. My dad had been working in Scotland."

No wonder I'd not seen her before.

"Nice to have you back," I replied, not knowing what else to say.

"Are you drunk?" she asked, a slight smirk on her face as she looked at me.

"That obvious, huh?"

"Ah, yeah, plus I know what an alcoholic looks like during the cold hard hours of the day," she said. Instantly, I saw the pain in her eyes as she looked to her feet. Someone was hurting her. I didn't know who she was, but instantly I wanted to hurt whoever thought they had the right to make that smile disappear.

"Thanks for saving me back there, Sloane. Ms. Campbell has it out for me."

"Well, you are a schoolkid and you're drunk," she giggled. "I can understand it."

"You're a kid, Sloane, you don't have to always make sense, you know. Now is the time for us to make mistakes."

"Why do you always say my name?" she asked me, her head cocked to the side.

The bell sounded to alert us to school starting.

"I like how it sounds," I admitted to her. She smiled at me, her cheeks slightly pink, before she headed toward her class. She turned around before she disappeared into the building.

"I hope I see you again, Killian."

She went through the door before I could form a response. Something funny was happening in my chest as I tried to stop my stomach from upending everything in it.

Who the fuck did I just meet?

I headed inside, through a separate entrance and announced to my History teacher that I was present. Ms. Allowrie grimaced as I took my seat in the back, before she marked me off in the registration and continued to watch me closely while she began to teach us about the history of Ireland. I ignored her for the majority of the class as I looked out the window and tried not to think about all the ways I could climb out the damn window and escape.

If I missed just one class, I knew my brother Lorcan would find out and I'd be in shit with my father. That was definitely not a place I wanted to be.

Today was going to be long, but I knew there had to be at least one class I would have with Sloane.

Surely, just one.

Then I could see those eyes again.

———

IT HAD BEEN a good two hours since I saw the beauty named Sloane. We were in third period and I could see her. She was laughing with her friends as she entered D block and headed up the same stairs I would need to ascend. I took a deep breath, hoping she'd be in the same class as me. As I entered the room for English, I saw her, sitting at the front with her friends. I took my usual spot at the back, that is, when I was in class. The teacher looked up from her desk to do her usual registration for the class and did a double take when she saw me.

"Mr O'Farrell, it's a pleasure to have you in my class again," she said, a slight smirk on her face.

"I figured I'd give you another shot at what you think literature should be," I shot back just as quickly. Her face turned from smugness to annoyance in no time flat. She knew she couldn't send me to the headmaster so she focused her attention on someone else.

Sloane was looking at me, as I shot my gaze over to her. She wasn't giggling like the other girls in class, in fact, she was looking at me like she was trying to figure me out. I almost felt uncomfortable with the way she looked at me but as the teacher moved to the front of the class, she broke our gaze.

I grimaced through the entire class as Ms Alden butchered her interpretation of Shakespeare. My mother would be horrified so hear this. She'd all had us taught before high school about Shakespeare. The bell rang to signal the end of class and we all headed out the door. Sloane was waiting for me in the hallway when I finally left.

"You didn't have to be so mean to the teacher," she chided me.

"Why are you so worried?"

"Are you just trying to be a bad boy and you have to offend everyone you see?" she asked me.

"I won't offend you," I told her before I pushed off the wall I had been leaning on and headed to the exit. My fascination with the new girl was over and it seemed my charm was wearing thin after too long in this damn place.

SLOANE

MY FATHER SLID the money into my hand to go in and pay for our dinner. He hadn't bought food or kitchen appliances since we returned to this town and this was the fourth night we'd had takeout. I was getting over the greasy burgers and cold fries but food was food. I headed past the group of kids from school who were mucking about in the parking lot, acting like they were king shit, and headed inside. I saw a few of the kids from school working the counters and the kitchen behind them. Ignoring the will to run and hide, I made my way to the counter and delivered my order.

My bored fellow student gave me the total in a monotone voice and took the cash. I moved to the side just as he called out to me.

"Wait, what's your name for the order?"

"Sloane Carpenter."

"Weird," he shrugged. "There's a Sloane Carpenter in my class."

I shrugged off the eye roll and wanted to shrink away before I responded. "Yeah, that's me."

He didn't have time to react before the next person was ordering. I waited in the corner of the room until he called out my name and handed me the bag.

"You sure you're in my class?" he asked me, with a sly smirk. "I would have noticed you."

"I guess the uniform makes me invisible to your kind," I replied, taking the bag and making a beeline for our car. A stranger stepped out in front of me, blocking my view. My father had always parked on the outskirts of the parking lot so it was easy to get home. But his view was blocked as to where I was at the moment.

Great.

"Where you going, pretty girl?" he slurred. I looked up into his eyes and could see the familiar glassy eyes of a drunkard. My uncle and grandfather had both been Grade A drunks so I knew this could get bad and fast.

"I'm heading to meet my father, he's just over there."

"He sends his little girl to fetch dinner alone?" he asked, moving closer to me, and causing me to back up. "That's not a good daddy. I'll look after you, little one."

The fear was rising in my chest and I felt my heart begin to hammer hard in my chest. I looked around for someone to help me but no one was daring to come and aid the new girl. The school kids had disappeared from before and the guys inside were busy. I could probably back up and head inside until my father came to look for me but I didn't want to give in like that.

"Problem, buddy?" I heard a familiar voice. The drunk turned around and backed up slightly.

"No, I was just asking the lady if she needed help."

"She doesn't," Killian said. "Beat it."

The drunk all but ran away from us and left me reeling. My heart rate was still racing as I looked at Killian. Those dark eyes drawing me in.

"Thank you."

"You're welcome, you shouldn't have needed help though."

He looked around at the other students who had started to come out. One of them, a boy I recognized as being on the school's football team, came over to us at a slight jog.

"Killian, I was just coming to her aid."

27

"I didn't see you," Killian replied. "Get lost, Draper."

The boy ran off, leaving me alone with Killian again.

"Why is everyone so scared of you?" I asked him, my voice all but breathless.

He smirked at me. "You should go, your food is getting cold."

I didn't wait around, knowing my father would come looking for me soon. I headed to the car and tried to get rid of the memory of those dark eyes.

One thing I knew for sure, Killian was going to be on my mind until I found out more about him.

I SHOT out of bed and grabbed my blanket, pulling it up to my chest to stave off the cold air. The memories coming back to me since he'd left here after kissing the hell out of me were not helping with my lack of sex life. I remembered that night, where he had saved me from possibly being raped or killed by a drunk, like it was yesterday. That was the night I knew I would do anything I could to be able to kiss those lips, have those dark eyes drink me in and never want another woman again.

It was the night, I knew I would never want another and that was just the first day I'd met him. Killian had always been the one.

I loved my husband, there was no doubt, but if Killian had come calling and not stayed away like he promised, I couldn't say for sure if I would have been loyal. I grabbed my dressing gown and headed to the kitchen to boil the kettle. The sun was still down, but I could feel it was morning, before I even checked the time. Killian was still very much on my mind as I put the teabag in the mug and waited.

I had to get over this shit. Killian was not the forever kind of guy. That much was for sure. I knew about his reputation around town. He'd bedded half or maybe more of the town, single or married. I knew that had been because of me, I'd broken his heart when I had realized we'd never be able to be together. His father had had too firm of a hold on him and I knew he was going down a dark path. One I couldn't follow him down.

Now, I was fantasizing about him, and it wasn't great for my poor, cobwebbed pussy which hadn't seen action since Sean had died.

She was ready to play and she wanted Killian.

I shrugged off the memories and poured the water into my mug before I steeped my tea bag and took it into my living area, putting the heater on before I pulled the blanket over my legs. I needed to finish cleaning this damn cottage and sell it before returning to work so I could fill my life with purpose again and finally stop thinking about Killian.

Ha, yeah right, Sloane.

Killian was back in your life, there was no way I was getting away from him again.

My pussy throbbed at the thought of having him down there again, all the while my brain was screaming for me to stop.

Those eyes would haunt me forever.

And in the back of my mind, I had that little glimmer of a voice saying, *What if you didn't break it off with him? What if you could have him now?*

Tears began to pool in my eyes as I sipped my tea and tried to will my brain to stop thinking about Killian fucking O'Farrell.

KILLIAN

I COULD FEEL the eyes on me, subtle and yet not so subtle at the same time. The music was loud and the club was packed but I could feel someone watching me. Usually, it didn't disturb me, I was an O'Farrell for one but I also owned the only club worth going to in this damn town. People wanted to get in my pants for one reason or another, a conquest on their little bingo card before they settled down into a life of misery with someone who would inevitably end up beating them or cheating on them.

It was the same old story, day in and day out. This town was poisonous, and it had slowly been drowning its people for the last few decades.

As I turned to one of my bar people, Asher, I motioned for a drink. He got to work on it immediately, no matter the large line waiting for their drinks. I looked around, hoping to catch who was watching me but it was the same old people who came here every weekend pretty much, although tonight was busier being a weekend and the fact I had booked one of the hottest Irish DJ's to play. My brother Conor was dancing with his woman Teeghan in the middle of the dancefloor, enjoying what fleeting moments they had together. He ran a tight ship down at the docks, and spent way too much time away from home but they made it work somehow. I was happy for him. Since Tee had come along, Conor had settled his reckless behavior down so much that I barely recognized the kid. Before her, we'd be calling constant family meetings at the estate to sort the shit he'd started with warring families. I couldn't count how many times I'd saved that fucker's life by bartering something important to our family to another family just to ease the tension.

Asher put my drink down in front of me and went back to the lineup of thirsty patrons. I headed up the stairs to my balcony that overlooked the dancefloor and every aspect of the club. I spent most of my time up here, usually with a woman who would do anything I asked her to. The darkness of the room behind the balcony, where I conducted business meetings with the underworld of Ireland, was usually where I had women do those unmentionable things to me. I eased into my chair and looked out at the party goers below, enjoying the fruits of my labor. Signing DJ Shamrox was not easy, and had taken some serious groundwork to get him here but here he was and my club was reaping the rewards. Out of all the businesses my father left to my brothers and I, my club was beginning to be more lucrative than ever and it was killing both my brothers.

I smiled into my drink as I thought of all the things Lorcan and Conor said behind my back.

Out of the corner of my eye, I saw movement in the room behind me. I put my drink down quickly and pulled my gun from my holster and entered through the glass sliding door. The room was draped in darkness, as I preferred, but I could see pretty quickly who had disturbed the peace.

I took a deep breath, and put my gun away, as I gazed upon the naked form of one of the girls who had taken an interest in me since she'd become of age.

"Sabrina, go home."

"Come on, Killian, don't you want a piece of this?" she asked, twirling her body around. I could see she had doused herself in glitter body gel and shined through the lights that danced into the room every now and then.

On any other night, I would probably have her kneel

down and give me what my cock so desperately needed but I couldn't feel even a little turned on right now.

Not when Sloane was so heavy in my mind.

"Sabrina, I'm not interested."

She seemed a little steamed, but it didn't force her to put her clothes back on, instead, she came toward me. Her hips sashaying over to me in a way that would normally have my cock jumping for joy but not tonight.

I was surprised myself, but not enough for me to undress and have the 18 year old up against the wall.

Before she could get to me, I grabbed her dress and panties from the side of the room and tossed them at her before I opened the door to the room which would lead down to the hallway that you either rejoined the club or left out the back door.

Sabrina's mouth told me she was about to make a scene. I ordered her out and she stomped over to me, like a child, and tried to lay a kiss on me. I moved away and she made a squeal that could have been made by a pig before she made her way down the hall. I turned, making sure she left, before I was about to head back into the room. That's when I saw Conor and Tee standing at the top of the stairs, huge grins on their faces.

"Not a fucking word," I said to them both. Conor stayed where he was, the grin of a kid on his face, while Tee made a motion of zipping her lip before she headed into the room. Conor slid past me, chuckling the entire way.

Just fucking great.

I clicked the button just inside the door to alert Asher to start bringing up drinks for the three of us and joined them out on the balcony.

"So, who was your friend?" Tee asked, a slight giggle in her voice.

"I thought you zipped your lip?"

"I decided to unzip it," she said with a smirk on her face that reminded me just how perfect she was for my little bro.

"She's just one of his little club bunnies," Conor said. "Never seen you kick one out naked before."

"Enjoy your night?" I asked them, hoping like hell they would drop it before I dropped them.

Tee and Conor were both laughing as Asher came into the room with a tray of glasses and a bottle of my best bourbon. He put it down on the table between us and exited just as quickly as he came in.

"Lorcan's joining us later," Conor announced as he poured his and Tee's drinks. Great, just what I needed, an impromptu family meeting at my club. I topped up my drink and waited for my phone to go off so I could have an excuse to leave. I didn't need Conor knowing about the shit with the English. He'd only run in half cocked like he always did and fuck it all up.

The only thing I could hope for was an emergency or a booty call that I didn't mind getting hard for tonight.

Staring at my phone, I begged God to save me.

CHAPTER THREE

SLOANE

Teeghan was late as usual. I sipped at my latte and looked down at my phone, playing a game of Solitaire while I waited. The day was brisk, colder than it was at the cottage, which was a nice change.

When my best friend finally turned up, I couldn't help but smile as I watched her sit down with a thud. Her thick black sunglasses were perched over her eyes, and her lips were still stained with last night's lipstick. She crossed her arms over her puffy jacket as she looked over at me.

"Have a good night?"

"Shut up," she grunted. "Get me a coffee, damn woman."

I motioned for our waiter to come over and take our order before she fell off her chair and fell asleep under the table. It reminded me of the early days when we would go out and party all night long and come to this cafe and try to sober up before returning home. My memories sobered at that, because more than once, I'd been kicked out by my overbearing mother for coming home a sloppy mess as she had called me. That's when I would call Killian to come and save me.

And he would.

Every damn time.

Even if it angered his father, he would come and take me away, to the beach, to a lake house...somewhere no one could find us for days.

"Earth to Sloane?"

I zapped the memory from my mind and focused on Teeghan who had finally removed her sunglasses. The waiter was waiting patiently for the order. I gave him my usual and he toddled off but that didn't stop the look crossing Teeghan's face.

"Who is he?"

"Oh shut up," I shot at her. "You know I don't have time for that."

"Please," she sighed, and lounged back in her chair. "You've all the time in the world. Whatever have you been doing down in that cottage for so long?"

"Packing it up," I told her. Her expression changed to one of curiosity.

She sat forward. "Really? You're going to sell it?"

I nodded. "Would that upset you?"

"No," she said quickly. "You've needed to move on for ages now. Do you need help? I could come down and help you."

"I appreciate the offer, honey, but I need to do it myself."

Tee nodded, understanding. I also didn't want her to find any knick knacks I hadn't gotten rid of from Killian. I didn't think I could explain that to her, after all, she was Sean's sister. I couldn't even explain it to myself.

"What did you and Conor do last night?" I asked her as our food arrived.

"We went to the club," she said. "DJ Shamrox was playing."

"Who?"

Tee rolled her eyes. "God, only the biggest DJ in Ireland, of course."

She was mocking me, I could tell. She didn't care an iota for DJ's, but I had no doubt someone of that caliber would be playing there. That club had been a thriving success since Killian took it over.

"Do you remember when we snuck in there just before we turned 18?" I recalled, with a chuckle. It had been before Killian took over from his father, and had been a miserable club. Hardly anyone went there, and those that did, were always criminals.

"Oh god, don't remind me. I'm pretty sure I drank my weight in vodka and needed a stomach pump."

I remembered the call to her father from the hospital and wanting to high tail it out of there before he got there. Instead, Sean had turned up to rescue his little sister before their parents found out.

That had been the night I'd met him.

"Good times."

"Not, good times, Sloane."

I laughed as I dug into my omelet.

"We hung with Killian most of the night anyway," she said. Just the sound of his name had my heart hammering in my chest. "Well, after we caught him kicking a naked girl out of the room."

Tee was laughing at the memory as my heart began to

throb, a sharp pain shooting across my chest. I knew he was a slut, sleeping his way through Ireland's women, but hearing about this naked girl had me feeling sick to the stomach.

Especially after the near miss a few days ago.

That should be enough to make me steer clear of him, but I knew better. I knew my heart wasn't going to be content until it was broken once again.

And by Killian of all people.

"Are you okay?" Teeghan asked.

"Yes, why?"

"You look a little pale," she said.

"I'm just over cleaning," I lied. "I'll be good in a few days when I'm done."

Tee bought the lie and went back to her coffee and food while I tried to rid images of that little smirk he always wore around me, and those devilish eyes from my mind.

I was losing the battle, and I knew it. There was only one way to get rid of this feeling.

One true way of seeing Killian for the whore he was.

I needed to surprise him, and catch him in the act with some hussy. Then I could hate him for making me feel this way again.

———

LATER THAT NIGHT

I wiped my sweaty palms down the sides of my dress as I stepped in through the door. The doormen had let me in, even though there had been people standing outside for hours. I wondered if he knew I was here.

But if he did, I would have seen him down on the

dancefloor waiting. Instead, I saw him up on the balcony, looking down at the club below with boredom.

Heading to the staircase that would lead up to the room, I ascended the stairs quickly. My heart was in my throat, as I made my way to the room and opened the door. The music from below didn't alert Killian to my entry.

I had come here for one thing and one thing only.

To shock and awe, and to give my heart something it was begging for.

A good fuck.

I slipped my panties down my legs and made my way over to him on the balcony. He got up quickly, his gun trained on me. Instantly my pussy began to throb, sheer panic shooting through me as he lowered the gun quickly.

"Sloane?"

I didn't respond, instead, I willed my legs to work again as I took control. I shoved him back down on the chair and straddled his lap. He laid the gun down on the floor beside him as he looked me up and down, those eyes darkening with desire.

I undid his jeans and maneuvered them over his hips while he was still sitting on the chair. He allowed me to take charge, and I found it exhilarating. I guided his cock into my already aching and wet pussy. The feeling of him filling me, had my mouth working itself into an O as I moved up and down, to get a feel for his girth, before I sat down on him fully, feeling my pussy wrap around him. His hands went directly to my hips to hold me on his lap as I began to ride him. His eyes didn't waver, they never left me as I took what I desperately needed from him.

The way he looked at me had me feeling things I didn't know I could feel again. To stop the gaze, I slammed my lips down onto his, wrapping my tongue around his and tangling for dominance. He groaned into my mouth which only did things to my clit as I continued to ride him.

His finger danced over my clit, and before I could stop him, he was rubbing it. My nerve endings were on fire as I screamed into his mouth as my pussy erupted around him. He groaned into me, his teeth scraping my tongue as I imagined my pussy strangled his cock.

I continued to move, up and down, as my pussy throbbed from my orgasm. He gripped my hips harder as he took control, my mouth slipping from his as he pulled my head down to his shoulder and he slammed his hips up, so I could feel his cock go even further than before.

The sheer brutality of his movement was enough to send me reeling as he exploded into me suddenly. I rode out every pump of his cock until finally we relaxed against each other in the chair, trying to catch our breath.

During the act, I hadn't cared if anyone could see us, but now, my fears laced through me like a spark of fire. I slid off him and steadied myself on the glass doors behind me. No one was looking up here and I looked over at Killian, his cock still out and wet.

"Sloane..."

He knew what I was going to do. I didn't have to say a word. He knew this was just a fuck and I was going to walk...if I could remember how to do it again. I turned my back to him and found my panties on the floor before I took off down the hall and out to the back door.

I prayed he didn't follow me, because I didn't think I could stop now.

My plan had failed.

I wanted him more than ever before.

Once wasn't enough.

I was well and truly fucked now.

Tears burned my eyes as I found a safe spot to put my panties back on before I got into my car and headed back to the cottage.

I was a fucking idiot.

KILLIAN

WHAT THE FUCK WAS THAT?

Since when did Sloane hit and quit it?

I wasn't complaining. I'd missed that wet pussy more than anything before. If anything she'd only gotten sweeter with age. The way she had ground against my cock had it getting hard again just at the memory.

Did she think I would treat her like one of the other women I fucked? No fucking way. I did up my jeans again and stood up. I needed to stop her.

The familiar feeling of being watched crept over me as I looked down to see one person looking up at me.

Amity.

Shit.

The smirk on her face told me she had seen what had just occurred up here and now she had plans. Plans that involved Sloane.

She knew how to hurt me.

Fuck.

Sloane wasn't safe. I had to get to her. I took off, grabbing my gun off the floor, and hightailing it to my car before I sped toward the cottage and to Sloane.

———

I THREW my fist against the door, causing it to rattle from the force. My mind was racing, my cock was already hard, actually I was pretty sure it hadn't gone soft since Sloane had fucked me on the balcony. He wanted her on a normal day, but after that diva move, it wanted her naked and under him more than ever. Sloane opened the door, her eyes wild with fear. Then she saw me.

"Killian, look, it was just a one time thing-"

I shoved past her, not wanting to hear it. She closed the door and turned to face me.

"You better lock it," I said.

"Why?"

"There's no way in hell I'm going to let anyone interrupt us," I said, removing my jacket and shirt before I closed the distance between us. I swept her into my arms, shoving her back against the door so I could lock it myself. She smelled just as sweet as she did in the club. Her soft moans were driving me wild as I pulled her up the door, holding her there with my thigh while I pulled her dress up and over her head, tossing it behind me. She had on a lace bra but I could see her puckered nipples behind the material. I took one of her breasts into my mouth, and sucked the nipple hard, using my teeth to scrape over the lace.

Sloane gasped and tried to pull away but I had her close. I undid the back of her bra and freed her breasts easily before she worked at my jeans again. I picked her up, her legs wrapped around my waist as I walked her into the room and toward the couch. Her arms wrapped around my neck as she laid her lips on mine and kissed me hard. My cock was aching for release as I pulled the tops of my jeans down enough to free him. He bounced up quickly and toward her soaking panties.

I pulled her down off my hips and turned her so she

was facing the back of the sofa. Leaning her over, I saw her ass cheeks looking primed for a spanking. The lacy material of her panties only just covered her ass crack. I smacked one cheek, relishing in her surprised gasp and the sound of my skin hitting hers. I grabbed the thin piece of lace covering her delicious pussy and I ripped it from her.

Sloane, again, gasped in surprise but she didn't move. In fact, she held onto the top of the lounge as I pushed my jeans off my legs and took hold of my cock, pushing it into her pussy from behind in one fell swoop until I could feel all of my cock was swallowed by her.

I grabbed her hair, and pulled her head back. Her neck stuck out as her back bowed and I could see her eyes looking up at me, searching for what I'd do next.

I kissed her hard as I pulled out of her and slammed all the way back in, removing my hand from her hair. She leant back down, her gasping turning into moans as I began to fuck her hard. I lifted one leg up so I could move more freely into her. She held onto her leg as I held onto her hips, keeping her in place as I fucked her for dear life.

I never wanted to be anywhere but here.

Just like I hadn't wanted another pussy back then, back when I had her as my girl.

I couldn't think about that now, or I'd never be able to be without her again. I'd never let her meet someone who could make her happy.

I focused on the job at hand, fucking her, and making her happy for now.

Now, that I could do.

God...how did she feel so fucking perfect? So fucking good as I slid in and out of her. It was like I was home.

As I heard her scream out, I felt her pussy walls begin to

squeeze my cock. It didn't take long until I was tumbling over into her myself.

Ashamed at how quickly she made me cum, I vowed I would make her cum at least five more times before the sun came up.

I was no two pump chump, and she damn well knew it.

SLOANE

MY THIGHS WERE ACHING as I rolled over onto my back, and opened my eyes, looking up at the ceiling of the cottage. I turned over but Killian wasn't there. His side of the bed was ice cold. I'd been such a light sleeper for most of my life, I don't know how I didn't hear him get up.

He must have snuck out like a ninja.

I didn't expect to feel hurt by it, after all, I had fucked him and left at the club. I'd had no intention of letting him fuck me in this cottage afterward but I'd been unable to say no.

My body reacted to his touch like it had that first time, and I knew it always would.

God.

Why had I let my life get complicated by the O'Farrell's again? I should have left, gone over to Dublin and taken that big job my cousin had offered me. I would have been free, able to move on properly and cut all the bad shit out of my life.

I got up and headed into the shower, to wash the remnants of last night off me. If I closed my eyes, I saw him, over me, as he slammed that cock into me over and over again. My pussy was betraying me again, wanting another round with the man.

I quickly finished up and got dressed. I was determined to finish this damn cottage so I could actually do something with my life other than wither away as a bitter old widow.

Grabbing an empty box from the side of the room, I taped the bottom to make it more sturdy and started to pack away the books I'd had in my family for generations. It was at this point, a knock landed on my door and startled the ever living hell out of me.

If that was Killian...

I made my way over to it and opened the door just as an unfamiliar man smiled at me.

"Can I help you?" I asked him.

"I'm here to collect you, miss."

"Collect me?" I repeated, my heart beat starting to race. "I'm not sure I understand."

"Sorry," he said. "Killian said you were to come with me so we could ensure your safety."

That son of a bitch.

"I'm quite safe here. I don't think getting into a stranger's car is going to be an action I'll take today. Thank you though."

"He said you would refuse," the man smirked before holding out a phone. I saw Killian's name on the screen as he pushed the speaker button.

"Get in the car, Sloane."

His voice was slightly irritated, and I could tell he was in no mood to play, but he was the one who left me alone in bed this morning. He could have simply taken me with him if he was so worried about my safety.

I mean...why would my safety be challenged? I wasn't part of their family.

"Coming from the man who left me alone this morning?" I yelled through the phone. "I'll kindly refuse. Thanks."

I closed the door in the guy's face before I changed my mind. He didn't knock again, and I felt as if I didn't breathe until I heard his car take off away from the cottage.

What in the everloving hell was this?

I chose a life away from Killian for a reason, all those years ago, and now here I was, back in it. This was exactly why I couldn't have chosen Killian.

He was full of danger.

And hot sexy nights like last night.

But mostly, I didn't want to end up like the women tended to in that family.

Dead.

I moved back over to the box I had been working on and continued to pack away the contents of the bookcase. Looking around, I could see I was about 90 percent done with the cottage. So many memories, so many years of hating this place and then loving it as I got older.

But I was back to hating it enough that I needed to sell it.

———

I FINISHED my coffee and put the mug in the sink. The entire cottage was in boxes. As I turned around, I saw that what I'd been putting off was done and I had no excuse but to start figuring out what I wanted to do with the rest of my life.

The knock on the door had me jumping, yet again.

Did this motherfucker seriously send his man back down here to come and get me?

How lazy could you get?

I marched over to the door and swung it open to launch a yelling match when I saw who stood there.

That fucking smirk on his face, just like his brother's.

"Conor, did he seriously think *you* could change my mind?" I spat at him.

"What's wrong with me?" he asked, but the smile on his face told me he wasn't offended.

"Seriously, after corrupting my best friend and having her stay in Ireland when she had plenty of prospects elsewhere? You think you're better than the one he sent here before?"

Conor sighed, but he wasn't offended. "I wouldn't have come at the behest of my brother if it weren't serious."

"How serious?"

"A grieving widow is blaming the family for the loss of her husband, and now she wants to hurt us. The only way she's getting to Killian is through you."

I sighed. "Jesus. I tried to be rid of you guys. It almost worked, and then you came along and cast your little spell over Tee and now I'm back in this bullshit all over again."

"It's not so bad, Sloane. Come on. Get your shit and let's go."

I rolled my eyes and turned to grab my things. If he sent Conor of all people here, it meant things were bad enough for him to send for me.

I was still mad though.

Once I got my bag, I locked up the cottage and got into his car. At least I could spend some time with Teeghan.

———

I SAT IN THE BACK, not wanting to engage with him. I'd never admit to him, but I honestly didn't find him that vexing anymore. Teeghan was happy, for the first time in... well, pretty much since I met her. She was content, and safe, but I'd continue my little attitude toward Conor as long as I could because I didn't believe Teeghan should be in the world he was in. Just like I didn't belong in it. No matter how much I had loved Killian back then, I couldn't betray myself by acting blind when it came to the things he did.

They called him the calm assassin for fuck's sake.

I knew you didn't get a nickname like that without being cold in some way or another. But Killian had always had something about him that was deadly. I knew that better than anyone. Even in school, the other students and even teachers respected him, and knew not to mess with him and eventually they didn't mess with me either. I'd been drunk on the power of it all, until I realized I had been losing a part of myself.

"Do you want music?" he asked me. It broke me from my silent reverie.

"Sure."

He pushed a button on his touch screen and music filtered through the car. Conor kept to himself as he drove me back into the city. I looked out the window at the coast-line, and wondered what if I had gone to Dublin when I'd had the chance.

What if...things with Killian could work out this time. I wasn't the same naive and innocent girl I was back then.

Maybe I could withstand the shit they did now. Maybe, just maybe, I could find peace with it all.

Or maybe I was lying to myself because I desperately wanted Killian between my legs again.

. . .

KILLIAN OPENED *the door to the lake house he'd taken me to the last time I'd had to escape from my drunk mother. He knelt in front of me as he lifted my chin with his finger. I tried not to look him in the eye as he inspected the bruises and cuts.*

"Are you okay?" he asked me. I finally looked into those black pits of his eyes, and the tears began to fall onto my cheeks.

"Yes."

"I'll kill her."

"No," I stopped him from going to do what I knew he would. I didn't want him behind bars. I wanted him beside me, stopping the next attack. "Please, Kill, stay here."

He sighed, but I could see the tension leaving his body as he turned back to me and finally he joined me on the edge of the bed.

"Did I interrupt you?" I asked him. "You didn't seem happy on the phone."

"I was in a fight with my dad."

"Oh," I said. He never told me about his family, especially not his mob boss dad who ran the entire town. "I'm sorry. You can go."

"No," he said. "I don't need to . Lorcan's his heir, not me."

I didn't like the way he said that, but I didn't want to fight. I just needed him to hold me. As if he knew that, he wrapped his arm around my shoulders and pulled me into his chest. I let the sobs wrack through my chest as his strong arm held me.

I felt so utterly safe with him.
I never wanted him to be away from me.
I didn't think I would survive.

. . .

"ARE YOU OKAY?"

I broke from my memory and looked over at Conor. He looked at me with concern. "I'm fine."

"Okay, well we're here."

I got out of the car and looked up at the grand estate. It was always so intimidating being here again. It was the only place like it in our city, being built when the town was discovered centuries ago. Teeghan ran out of the double doors and into my arms. It felt so good to have her wrap her arms around me. I could feel her positive energy and it was lifting my spirits, which was always welcome.

"You look like you could use a cocktail," she said. "Come on."

I entered through the doors and took in the grand foyer. This place had once been a safe haven for me back in the day, and hopefully I could feel that same sense of safety I had once felt with Killian while this whole thing blew over.

Whoever this bitch was that was after them, she would soon see that I was noone to Killian and she'd leave me be.

"Where's Killian?" I asked Conor as he joined us inside.

He sobered a little, looking to Tee first, then back at me. "Oh, he's in Belfast actually. Urgent business. He'll be back tomorrow morning."

"So where am I staying exactly?"

"In a guest room," he said. "Don't worry, Walt's done it up real nice. You have non stop bar service and food service here, Sloane. Maybe you won't hate me so much after your stay."

"That's asking a lot of the alcohol and food, Conor," I shot back. Conor let out a howl of laughter as he left me with Teeghan. She led me down a hallway, until we got into a room with a bar cart full of alcoholic drinks and a library of books. I'd never been in this room before.

I fought back the irritation that Killian wasn't even here after he had taken me from my cottage but I had my girl, and we had alcohol.

Fun times would be had.

And then when he finally showed his face, I could be mad.

CHAPTER FOUR

KILLIAN

My phone dinged in my pocket. I pulled it out to see my brother's name pop up.

CONOR

She's at the estate with Tee. She's safe but she's pissed. You owe me, bro.

KILLIAN

Thank you. I'll be back tonight.

I put my phone on silent and left it in the car as I took my backup, Liam and Tommy, into the house to meet with a contact who could help me reach out to the fucker who was trying to fuck up my business. I was close now.

I could end this before it turned into anything and then I could have Lorcan appreciate the fuck out of me instead of turn into Dad and tell me I should have had it handled before it even came to Ireland.

The fucker had never been happy which is why I think

Lorcan was never happy. He had the world on his shoulders. Lately, though, he'd been different. I wondered if a woman had breached the stony exterior of his and melted whatever was holding his heart hostage.

Liam and Tommy opened the door and I entered through it, with them at my back. My contact, Shannon, was sitting at the table, his own men behind him. His gun was trained on me under the table from his position.

This would be hostile, after all.

"Shannon."

"Sit down, Killian."

Shannon had once been in Lorcan's employ until he'd tried to rape some of the women he was supposed to be protecting. Lorcan hadn't been too happy, and had ordered a hit on him, but he was protected by someone now. Someone who called off the hit somehow.

It was all starting to bug me that this low life was still around and that he had contacts that could hurt our business at home.

"I heard you lost an important enemy," Shannon said as I sat down.

"And that would be?"

"Ronan, of course."

"Ronan is an idiot," I shot out quickly. "He's a marked man, Shannon. I wouldn't be building alliances with him."

"I was a marked man once, too."

"Am I here to talk about the past or am I here to talk about your contact?" I asked him, trying to get some control over the conversation.

I was desperate to get back home, and to Sloane. Leaving her in bed this morning had been the hardest thing I'd had to do for a while. Not only had I only had a few hours sleep thanks to both of us needing carnal pleasure over and over again, but I wanted to repeat it.

What was happening to me?

I never wanted to repeat it with a woman.

And I damn well never wanted to think about a woman when I was conducting business like I was supposed to be doing now.

"My contact wants to do a deal."

"I'll speak with him directly."

"No go," Shannon said with a smirk. I was about to wipe it off his face if he didn't give it up. "My contact will only speak with me."

"No deal."

I got up to leave when Shannon's men turned their guns on me. Liam and Tommy pulled their weapons and trained them on his men.

"Whoa," Shannon stood up, putting his gun down on the table. "Let's not get out of control here. I'm trying to help you, Killian."

"No, Shannon, you're trying to help yourself. You think this contact can save you? You may have momentarily had power, but you won't have it forever. We will find out who is doing this and we will prevail. Like we always do."

Shannon made a move to grab his gun just as I pulled mine from my holster and shot him in between the eyes. His men could barely believe it before Liam and Tommy took them out before they got a shot off.

"Shit."

"Grab his phone," Tommy told Liam. We took their phones and tossed the house to make it look like a robbery. Exiting out of the house, I got into the car with Liam and Tommy.

"He mentioned Ronan," Tommy said.

"Yes," I replied. "That fucker has his finger in this."

"We haven't been able to find him for months. Can we ask his brother?"

"I will," I told them. "He doesn't know everything but he does know some things. Maybe we need to pick up the trace on Ronan again before we lose him and he gets more of an army to take us over."

I nodded and took off, back toward our city. My mind was racing. If Ronan was behind all of this, it would make sense, but how could he gather that much power in such a short amount of time? It was impossible.

Or was it?

Surely there was a way to find out.

SLOANE

"WHAT IS THIS?" Teeghan asked as I moved the portrait and showed her the secret passageway I had used when Killian and I were hiding from his father after he had snuck me in late one night.

"It's a place we could hide so we could be together."

"Wait...you and Killian fucked in here?"

"No," I rolled my eyes even though she couldn't see it. "We made out a bit, but never got carnal."

"So you know this estate better than me?"

"I know where Killian showed me. I wasn't here all that much and I usually only saw his bedroom."

"It's still so crazy to think of you and him together."

"Tell me about it."

"What was he like back then?"

"Strangely enough, exactly as he is now. Killian hasn't changed much, maybe he's just a little more intense."

"I can't imagine that. He's always so sure of himself... unless he's trying to get rid of me because he thinks I'm trying to hurt his little brother. Now that was plain scary."

"Scary Killian is why I broke up with him," I told her, putting my empty glass down on the tray. "I couldn't be with someone who could easily kill a bunch of men then come home to me. I mean, where did that end and the real Killian start?"

Teeghan poured another drink but I put my hand over my glass. "I'm beat, I'll have Walt show me to my room."

Teeghan hugged me tightly and let me leave without complaint. She wouldn't be able to resist calling Conor down to the room to have her way with him soon. I knew what she was like with alcohol in her system.

Walt was all too happy to show me to my room as I took in the modest guest room. "Anything you need, you holler."

I thanked him and closed the door before I sat on the edge of the bed and thought about all the bad things that could happen by me staying here.

And...all the good things.

KILLIAN

WALT TOLD me which room she was in and told me she had retired about two hours ago but I knew she wasn't asleep. Sloane could never sleep in a strange bed unless she was drunk or drugged...or with me.

I took the stairs two at a time before I opened the door slightly. Sloane was sitting by the window, looking out at the view below.

"About time you showed up," she said. She was tired, I could see it in her eyes and hear it in her tone.

"I see Teeghan got you stuck into the good liquor."

"She did," Sloane said, putting her mug down on the windowsill. "She always did know how to show a girl a good time."

"I'm sorry I had to leave," I told her. "I had urgent business in Belfast."

"Conor said you wouldn't be home until tomorrow."

I nodded, reminding myself I needed to choke the hell out of Conor for opening his trap. "Things didn't go to plan."

"I know what that means," she replied. "I'm tired, Killian. I don't think I can manage to understand what you're telling me right now."

I nodded again. "I just wanted to make sure you got here all right."

"How long am I being held captive?" she asked me, a weariness in her tone.

I felt the anguish in her voice, and it only made me feel like the jerk I was being even more.

"You're not fucking captive, Sloane. You can leave when you want but it's just safer here until we can sort her out."

She nodded and moved to the bed to get under the covers. I desperately wanted to join her but I could see she was too annoyed to let that happen.

"Sweet dreams, Sloane."

"Just go," she said softly, but it felt like daggers in my chest as I left the room and exited down the hall to my old room. I'd cleared the stuff out when I had moved to my apartment, so now it just looked like a regular guest room, but the memories of what happened in this room were still ever present in my mind.

The only girl I had ever brought home was Sloane.

And it would remain that way.

Hopefully with a good night's sleep, she would change her mind and she would see this for what it was.

A safety precaution.

I doubted Amity could pull anything off but I couldn't risk Sloane.

CHAPTER FIVE

SLOANE

I headed for the door just as Conor rounded the corner and tried to stop me.

"I am not in the mood for you, right now. Get out of my way."

"Sloane, staying here...it's for your own good."

"Remove yourself from my view, Conor, or so help me I will cut your dick off."

Conor's smile eased and he looked concerned. He knew I would too. I'd been cooped up in this damn house, with someone at my beck and call the entire time. I hated it. I was not used to this treatment and I didn't like not being able to do simple things like go out into town and do what I wanted to do.

"Let her go, Conor."

I turned to see Lorcan leaning against a doorway, and I could see he'd aged since I last saw him. I always liked Lorcan, he was smart and intelligent and always covering for his brother's.

Conor begrudgingly moved away from the door and let me walk through it. I realized now that I'd let Conor drive me.

I was stuck here and it was a long ass walk down the driveway until I got into the town center.

Fuck.

"I'll drive you."

I turned to see Lorcan heading toward the garage. Within moments, he pulled up beside me in his car. I got in and let him take me down to the city.

"Cottage or here?" he asked.

"Town," I told him, wondering how he knew about the cottage or the fact that I had been staying there. "I need to get some supplies."

"I can wait."

"It's okay," I told him. "I'll find my way back down to the cottage."

Lorcan was hesitant and for a moment, I didn't think he would unlock the car but he did after a brief pause. I got out and closed the door. He waited until I got into the grocery store before he took off.

I felt like I could take a breath of air for the first time for days. Being close to Killian for days but not actually allowing him to be around me had been hard. My pussy had been screaming for me to forgive him and let him in, and yet my heart knew better. My head was finally listening to my heart and telling me to keep my distance.

"Sloane Carpenter," I heard my name being called out. Pushing Killian out of my mind, I turned to see a familiar face. One I hadn't seen in years.

"Oh, Amity," I gasped. "It's been forever and a day."

She came over to me and we hugged. It felt a little stiff

on her end, but she'd never been great with affection, even when we had been best friends in high school.

"Tell me about it," she chuckled. "I wanted to reach out after Sean died but I didn't quite know what to say."

"Oh, that's okay, it's been years now."

"I know," she said. "But, well, you know."

"What's been happening with you?" I asked her, wanting the awkwardness to go away.

"Oh, that's a long and sordid story. I wouldn't want to bore you."

"Am, don't be ridiculous. We've known each other since we were kids. Let me just grab a couple of things and we can head down to the cottage."

"The cottage?" Amity exclaimed. "Wow, you still have that place?"

I remembered back to the days when Amity and I would get her older brother to take us down there while my parents were too blitzed to know where I was, and we'd drink all of my mother's vacation liquor. We almost ended up in hospital the first time and my liver never fully forgave me for it.

"Sure do, actually, I'm looking to sell it if you know anyone."

She shook her head, and I could tell she was a little distracted, looking around. She must have a lot to talk to me about if she was nervous. I quickly grabbed enough things for a few days and headed to the cashier.

"I don't have my car," I told her, realizing now that I probably should have worked that out before now.

"That's okay, I have mine. This way."

I followed her to the car park behind the grocery store and we headed down the coast toward my cottage, singing to the same old songs we grew up on.

"This place hasn't changed at all," she said, as she looked at the cottage from her windscreen.

"Come on," I said, leading her to the door. I put the groceries down and started to pour chips into a bowl. Grabbing a bottle of wine, I put two glasses down on the table followed by the bowl of chips. Amity was looking around the cottage, as if she was waiting for someone to jump out.

"So," I said after a good few moments of silence. "What's been happening in your world?"

"I don't know if you know but I was married a few years ago," she said, taking a sip of the wine.

"Oh you were? Congratulations, I had no idea."

She smiled, but there was a pain behind it. I had a bad feeling this wasn't going to end up being a happy ending.

"Did you ever think about leaving Sean for Killian?"

I was surprised by the change of topic and the mention of Killian.

"Uh, no," I said. "I didn't think about leaving Sean for Killian. Kill and I were done by that point."

"But you still love him, right?" she asked, still standing up.

"I'll always love him but I'm not in love with him."

Liar, liar, my brain screamed out.

"You know what we're missing," I got up from the table. "Dip. I know I have some here somewhere."

I opened the bag from the grocery store and pulled out the tub of French Onion dip. I dropped the plastic lid on the kitchen floor and bent to pick it up.

"My husband died because of the O'Farrell's," Amity said, her voice deeper, more menacing. That's when I realized why she was asking about Killian.

She was the widow who was angry at Killian.

She wanted to hurt him.

I dropped the dip, the creamy contents spilling all over the floor. Turning around, I saw her standing there, a gun in her hand, trained on me.

My fear was in my throat as I tried to back up.

"Why?" was all I could manage out.

"He loves you," she said, coldly. "I've seen what he would do for you, and honestly, I want him to hurt. It sucks that it has to be you, but Sloane, I think you know what it feels like to hate the O'Farrell's."

She was wrong.

I never hated them.

"You're going to kill me?"

Amity shrugged her shoulders as if my life were already forfeit. Tears began to well in my eyes as I thought of never having kids, never being able to tell Killian that I hated that I still loved him.

"I hope it doesn't come to that, and knowing Killian, he may well do whatever I ask for you. That way he can pay with his life, and not yours. For now, I need to take you away from here. Be a good girl and get in the car."

I backed up, trying to reach for my bag but Amity shot at my hand. It didn't hit me, but I felt the heat from the shot as my bag fell to the ground.

"Not a fucking chance," she said. "Get in the fucking car, Sloane."

I quickly moved to the car, hoping like hell one of my neighbors would see but I knew instantly they wouldn't. The only neighbors we had around here were holidayers. These cottages stayed empty during the winter.

No one was going to save me.

Why hadn't I stayed with Killian at the estate? Why had I left?

God damn it. Of all things to make the wrong decision about...it had to be this.

Amity shoved me to the back of the car and lifted the boot.

"No, please. I'll be okay. Just let me sit in the car."

"Does it look like I'm the same Amity from school?" she asked me. "You are collateral right now. You aren't even human to me. Get in or I'll shoot you."

I got into the boot, and she shoved my knees in at an odd angle before she shut the lid. I wanted to scream but I knew that would do no good.

The car hummed to life and we were taking off.

Off to my doom.

KILLIAN

I STOOD in the dining room, looking down at my brothers, feeling the fury rise. I'd never felt so red hot angry at them before, not even when we'd been younger and had close to hated each other.

"You let her go."

Lorcan stood up and I turned my attention to him. "I drove her to the town. She wanted to get back to her life, Killian. It's not her fault you can't control one pissed off woman."

My fist balled and I clocked him in the jaw. He barely moved from the action, but he also didn't retaliate.

"Feel better?" he asked me, as he turned his head back to me.

"Not in the slightest," I replied. Conor stood up, the little weasel, and tossed back the rest of his whiskey.

"Tee might know where she went. I'll ask her."

He left the room before I could launch across the table at him. My head was pounding, my chest was twisted up. I felt like I couldn't breathe.

"Sloane didn't want this life, Killian. You let her walk away all those years ago, why can't you let her live her life now?"

"I can, and I will," I told him. "But I can't have her hurt because of some bitch having issues coming to terms with the guilt over her husband's death."

"Guilt?"

"Yes," I said. "She's guilty because the night he died, she was with me."

Lorcan groaned, the same disapproving look Dad had when I'd done something stupid appearing on his face. Some days, he looked just like him.

"Jesus, Killian," he said, almost under his breath but I heard him clear as day. "Can you control your dick for just a few hours?"

"It's not my fault women want it," I shot back at him, annoyed he was making this my fault. "You could blame fucking Conor, he's the one who walked into an ambush that caused this shit."

"When you went over there to tell her...what did she do?"

"A lot of crying, a lot of wailing," I told him. "Then she took her clothes off and mounted me."

"So she slept with you after as well?"

I shrugged. "Nothing out of the norm for me. She's a fiery minx. She cried after it as well. That was when it got weird."

"No shit," Lorcan spat. "She was fucking grieving and you took advantage of her."

"If anything, she took advantage of me."

Lorcan threw the crystal bowl full of nuts at my head, narrowly missing me and landing against a wall and shattering to the carpet below.

"What the fuck?" I launched out of my chair.

"Have some fucking respect for her," he said. "She lost her fucking husband and you let her take her anger and sadness out on you but not in the way she should have."

"Would you have turned down a grieving widow in her time of need?" I asked him.

"Yes," Lorcan replied. "Because she didn't need the confusion sleeping with you would have caused her."

"Obviously, you're a better man than I am."

I turned on my heel and walked out to my car, so I could try and locate her myself. Maybe I was being overly cautious but after seeing Amity's house for sale and her business folded, I could tell she was setting herself up for something big.

No connections.

I started my car and was about to turn away when I saw the doors open and Conor come running out, Teeghan at his heel. I pushed the button to let my window down.

"What?"

"She's not answering anything," Teeghan said, worried. "She never ignores calls and messages. Her phone is going straight to voicemail."

The panic I had been experiencing before returned. I picked my phone up and dialed her number. An hour ago, it hadn't been going to voicemail. It had just been ringing out.

"Get in," I told them. They both eagerly jumped in the car. Teeghan in the back and Conor on the passenger side.

I sped down to the cottage as fast as I could with no complaints from Conor or Teeghan. I could see her in the rearview mirror, as worried as I felt.

Nothing had better happened to her or I would personally take Amity apart, limb by limb.

As I pulled into her driveway, I noticed the door hadn't been locked.

"Her car's still here," Teeghan said.

"I took her to the estate, remember," Conor told her. He grabbed his piece out just as I pulled mine from my holster and we kicked the door in. I moved in through the small cottage, looking at the spoiled dip on the kitchen tiles, the two glasses and a bottle of wine, the bowl of chips on the middle of the table.

"She was entertaining someone," Conor said. I looked through the bedroom but nothing had been disturbed in there.

"You know," Teeghan said, picking up her bag and pulling her phone out. It had been shut off for lack of charging. "She and Amity went to school together."

"Amity pretended to be her friend, probably drove her home, and then when Sloane put it together, she took her."

I looked to Conor, and realized he was probably right. Amity had Sloane.

"Where could she go?" I asked, but it wasn't directed at anyone in particular.

"Amity has family in Dublin."

"She wouldn't take her that far away. She's using her as a pawn."

"Go to the motor vehicles registry and try and locate her car on CCTV."

"Why the hell would they help us?"

Teeghan cocked her head to the side as if I had just asked a very stupid question. "You think you guys are the only ones with contacts? Sloane and I both know someone who works there and he would help us if I asked him to."

"He?" Conor and I both said in unison.

Teeghan rolled her eyes. "Guys, seriously. We have more important things to do right now than discuss who I or Sloane may be keeping friends with. Especially Sloane since she's not dating you, Killian."

Even though it were true, it still slapped me hard in the chest.

"Fine," I said. "Let's go."

Teeghan and Conor piled into the car first, just as I was about to shut the door and noticed the bullet hole.

Fuck.

———

"WELL, WELL, WELL, TEEGHAN KENNEDY," the guy smirked at her as he leaned over his desk at the RSA. "Look at you bringing your bodyguards in here. No matter what you say, I'm not getting rid of CCTV evidence of you speeding...again."

"Again?" Conor repeated.

The guy laughed and sat back into his chair. "What can I do for you?"

"Broge, I really need your help," she said. I noted the name on his name pin as Brogan. His smile disappeared and he leaned in again.

"What's going on?"

"I need you to track a car through CCTV."

"Teeghan...you know I can't do that."

"This bitch has Sloane and she means her harm," Teeghan said. Brogan's expression changed instantly.

"Right, who is she?"

"Amity Pearson."

"Amity Nolan," I corrected. "She was married."

"I know her," Brogan said. "Tracking her car now, it might take a few minutes. Go and wait outside, I'll meet you by the back staff door."

He put his "Closed" sign on his bench and we headed back outside. I had so many questions. How did Sloane know this Brogan guy, and how the hell didn't I know everyone she knew? I'd been her boyfriend for almost three years.

Teeghan was watching me as we waited, her head cocked to the side and slight smirk on her face.

"Just turn away, Kennedy."

She chuckled, knowing I was feeling jealous. Me...jealous...that was a new feeling and I really didn't fucking like it.

The door opened and Brogan held out a piece of paper to Teeghan. "She has a property a few towns over that she bought recently. Looks like she was heading that way the last time our cameras picked her up."

"Any sign of Sloane in the car?" Conor asked.

"No," Brogan said. "She was alone."

That was disappointing, but it was a lead. I desperately needed to find Amity and talk her down.

"Thanks Brogan," Teeghan said. He finally looked over at me, and saw that I hadn't taken my eyes off him. "You don't need to worry about Killian. He's harmless."

"That's not what I've heard," Brogan said. "If I weren't so terrified of your reputation, I'd be flattered, but you're not exactly my cup of tea, cupcake. I like my men skinny and dark, just like my coffee."

Teeghan laughed loudly as Conor led her away from the door and toward the car. Brogan hightailed it inside before I opened my mouth to speak. I was surprised that I hadn't realized he was gay until right now, but even then, I was still curious how he knew Sloane.

I headed back to the car. Conor had entered the address into the GPS by the time I started the car. As I pushed the button for the music to come on, we sped down to where Amity had bought property.

This had to have been a plan for the last couple of months. She'd not be able to pull this off in just a few weeks. What the hell had twisted in that girl's brain for her to do this?

Sloane wanted no part of my world and here she was twisted all up in it.

Fuck.

I knew better. I should have stayed away. I should have let her get on with her life.

But something inside of me knew there was no way I could let her walk away again, not this time.

SLOANE

MY HEAD WAS THROBBING when I opened my eyes. I prayed it wasn't one of my silent migraines. They were the actual worst and I was pretty sure I had packed away my Nurofen already. My surroundings were different, and for a brief moment, I failed to remember where I was.

That's when it hit me. I put my hand up to my head and felt the bump and the crusted blood from where Amity had split me open with the butt of the gun when I had tried to pounce on her once she'd opened the trunk to let me out.

I had no idea how long I'd been out or where I was, but I knew it had to be far away from home. There was no way she would risk keeping me in a town run by the O'Farrell's.

I got off the bed and looked around. The room was furnished, as if this was an actual house and not some run down abandoned shack. She was hiding me in plain sight.

The windows were bordered up, but there was a sliver or two through the boards she had nailed into the wall. There was just enough sunlight to tell me it was day.

I groaned as I sat back down on the bed. There was no way I could get out of this on charm alone. I needed to find out what she wanted so I could survive. I'd watched true crime documentaries. I knew the reason people didn't blindfold you.

Waiting was not exactly my strong suit, and I was desperate to find a way to get back home.

"Amity," I called out, banging on the back of the door. "Amity, come in here. I want to talk."

I stepped back, wondering if she would try and knock me out again. She unlocked the door and stepped inside, closing it behind her. I noted it was still unlocked but instead focused on her.

"It took you long enough to wake up," she said. "Sit down. We have things to talk about. I don't want to hurt you anymore. It's not you that I'm angry with."

"You hate Killian," I said. "I get it, he can be an asshole, but I don't see why you need me?"

Amity smiled, but it was almost an evil smile, one with no humor behind it. "I don't know how someone as intelligent as you are, can fail to see why you're being used. Surely, you know Killian would do anything for you."

"That was almost a decade ago, he sleeps his way around Ireland, surely someone else would make a better hostage."

I was fooling myself. Even I knew Killian never formed attachments, not since me, anyway.

"If you don't like him, why do you continue to be around him?" Amity asked me.

It was a curious question, one I wish I knew the answer to myself.

"Why do you care if you hate him?" I diverted the attention back to her.

Amity moved over to me, until she was face to face with me. I could see the dark eyes, the emotionless gaze she was giving me. It gave me chills.

She was no longer the girl I knew in school, she was a complete stranger and she was holding me hostage over some kind of feud with the O'Farrell's. Knowing how most of the O'Farrell's friends and family ended up, I knew I was a dead girl, all I could do was hope I could talk her out of it.

"Look, Amity, please, maybe I can help you. I can talk to them. You tell me what you want, and I'll get them to give it to you."

"You still don't get it," she said, shaking her head. I was trying to figure out what there was to get but before I could do that, I felt her hand come flying across the side of my face. The whack took me to my knees, the side of my face that was hit was burning with pain. "You're not here because I hate him. You're here because you're in the way."

She left the room, slamming the door shut and locking it again. I felt dizzy as I pulled myself up using the bedpost until I was sitting on the edge of the bed.

What the hell?

How the hell had I gotten it so wrong? Amity didn't hate him. She liked him and she wanted him all to herself. I had a pained feeling shoot across my chest at the thought. The last time that had happened was just after we broke up and I saw him with another girl.

Was I jealous?

Whether I was or not didn't matter. All I knew was she wasn't going to sucker Killian into liking her back.

This bitch was going down.

———

"ARE YOU SURE?" *Killian whispered in my ear. I could hear how excited he was, and I could feel it pressing against my leg as he lay half on his side and half on me. His bedroom was large, and looming, and the idea of his brothers coming in at any time was a little disconcerting. We'd left my friends downstairs to drink more and party while we snuck away. I was both excited and nervous as hell. I knew Killian was experienced. He'd been with girls before, and although that made me jealous as all get out, I had him now.*

"Yes," I whispered back. "Hurry up, before they find us."

Even though it was dark in the room, I could see the shadow of his face through the moonlight shining through the window. He was smiling, and it calmed me like nothing else in this world.

He bowed his head, his lips drifting across mine. He put his hand up to the side of my face, his calloused fingertips causing a ripple of friction that coursed through my body. He slid his hand down over my breasts, tickling my hardened nipple. His tongue tangled with mine, and I felt a sudden warmth spread over me, and inside of me. My nerves felt like they were on fire, my pussy was throbbing and I could finally understand what they meant by "getting wet". It felt oddly uncomfortable, and I didn't want him to go down there. I didn't want him to feel that.

I tried to shift my body away so that I could hide the fact that I was so wet down there but he had a strong hold of me. His lips left mine and he started to trail his way down to my neck. When his tongue traced a pattern on my neck, I felt my hips buck of their own volition and a moan escaped from my throat.

Killian's hand moved down my body, and pulled my panties away. I could feel the cool air hit my wet pussy and I gasped in surprise. Killian moved lower, putting his fingers over my pussy, diving in between my labia and starting to rub along the wetness on either side.

Without warning, his finger slid into me. I felt the pressure building as he tried to go further. My body was pulling away from him, I could feel myself moving up on the bed.

"Relax," he said softly.

I did, somehow, I found a way to relax as he slowly moved his finger around inside of me. The pain was there, but not to the extent it had been earlier. I could feel myself starting to enjoy the sensation of his finger massaging me from the inside. My hips began to roll around, my legs becoming active as I moaned out his name.

That seemed to spark something in him and he pulled down his pants. I looked, but couldn't see him in the dark as he nudged my legs wider. My heartrate picked up, right as he looked at me and moved in between my legs. I could feel his hard cock next to my leg as he leaned down and kissed me. I was so wrapped up in the kiss that I almost didn't realize what he was doing. His hand moved down between us. I felt a push and then the most excruciating pain as he pushed into me. He was slow at first, moving in and out, getting deeper and deeper with every push. I gasped as he hit my hymen and the pain that exploded inside of me took my breath for a moment. Killian took his time, making my comfort his priority. I loved him for that, even though I was sure this was probably killing him.

"I'm okay," I said, my voice crackly. "Keep going."

He kissed me again, and I melted into it, pushing the pain from my mind. He slowly moved into me again, and although it hurt, it was getting less painful with every move.

After a few more pumps, I could feel myself becoming more and more wet. I was starting to enjoy this. I moaned as Killian continued to pump into me, a strained look on his face.

"What's wrong?" I asked him, concerned I was hurting him.

He grunted but didn't say anything. My concern was quickly washed away as he pumped harder into me, sweat beading on his skin.

One more pump and Killian was groaning, as he pulled out from me and came onto the bed. I felt a little weird with him looking like he was in pain but I didn't think he was. My pussy was aching, but I knew it was in a good way.

"Are you okay?" he asked me.

"Yes, are you?"

"Yeah," he chuckled softly. "I'm great."

I moved off the bed and went into the bathroom. I looked at my hair all over the place in the mirror and the way my body looked. I was flushed from our activity and I could see the blood on my inner thighs.

I'd read about that, but it hadn't seemed to concern Killian.

I grabbed a bunch of toilet paper and wet it with water before I wiped away the remnants of my first time. Now that it was over, I couldn't wait to do it again. I finished up and moved back to my clothes. Killian was already dressed. His shirt was still off though.

"Did you enjoy it?" he asked me. I could see the genuine concern on his face and in his voice.

"Yes, at first not so much but it got better."

"Good," he replied. "Next time it'll be even better."

I moved into his arms. He tilted my head up and kissed me. It wasn't a hard or passionate kiss, it was a soft and tender one. One that promised much more than I could imagine. One that was hard to believe this was Killian, the son of the ruthless mob boss that ran our town, and who was grooming Killian to be just like him.

Not on my watch, I thought.

His hands were moving up and down my back, promising a round two was on the cards. I moaned into his mouth as he deepened the kiss and edged me toward the bed again. My pussy began to throb for him, wanting more.

"Sloane, are you in he-"

We both looked over to the door to see Amity standing there, shocked. It took her a moment before she exited without another word.

Killian and I both laughed.

"You should go," he told me. "She may need you to restart her heart after that."

I chuckled as I headed out the door to see what Amity had wanted. She was at the top of the staircase when I called out to her. When she turned around, I saw something in her eyes that looked like she'd been horrified.

"What's up?"

"I was wondering where you were," she said quickly. "I didn't know you and Killian were-you know...doing that yet."

"Tonight was the first time," I said, rather proudly. "But I can guarantee you, it won't be the last time if you know what I mean."

"Okay," she held her hand up. "I don't think we need to talk about it."

I was put off by her reaction. We'd never shied away

from telling each other things in our lives. I guess, sex had never been a factor until now.

"I'm just going to go," she said, as she started to head down the stairs. I was confused, as she headed to the door and outside.

Had seeing us together really upset her that much?

I couldn't imagine why.

I WOKE up from my memory dream and sat on the edge of the bed. Realization washed over me, almost to the point I was going to throw up.

She'd not been upset, she'd been jealous. Amity had never been shy about telling me about her sexual exploits either before or after that night, and yet, that was the night our friendship had become strained. It wasn't long after that when we parted ways, becoming polar opposites of each other.

Had this been going on all this time?

Had she been obsessed with him?

If she had been married, why would she be so obsessed with Killian now? None of this made sense.

One thing I knew for sure, I needed to stop Killian from coming to save me. If he even knew I was missing.

God, I was so stupid.

He'd been looking after me, in the wrong way, but he'd been trying to protect me and I had just marched on out and tried to resume my life.

But I knew...I knew more than anything that there was no life without Killian in it. I'd been living in a fantasy world thinking he wouldn't impact me again.

He'd always impacted me since that first meeting in school.

The door opened and Amity entered. I subconsciously backed up on the bed, waiting for her to attack me or do something to harm me in some way. Instead, I saw her hands move in front of her, a brown bag dangling from her fingertips. She threw the bag down on the end of the bed.

"I brought you food."

"How do I know you didn't poison it?" I asked her.

"Why would I?" she asked, annoyed. "If I wanted to kill you, I would have just shot you. I still need you for a reason. So eat."

"I get it now," I told her. "I get that you want Killian... but why? Why didn't you say anything earlier?"

Amity's guard seemed to lower a little. "You came to town, and you wrapped him around your finger. I'd been slowly chipping away at his coat of armor for years. I was close and then you come in with your perfect hair and your perfect smile and his attention was cast to you. Even after you broke his goddamn heart, he still loved you."

"I can't help that he never loved you back," I told her. That seemed to anger her but she didn't lash out at me. Instead, she simmered her rage and left, locking the door behind her.

The food did smell good, and she was right, she had a gun. She could easily shoot me if she wanted me dead.

Or...she could poison me and watch me die slowly.

Either way, my stomach was burning with hunger and if I didn't eat soon, I would pass out. I moved over to it and began to eat, trying to figure out a way to get away or perhaps, get a message to Teeghan that Killian was in danger if he came here.

KILLIAN

WE PULLED up outside the house. It had no neighbors, just land on either side of the older style house.

Teeghan and Conor were both pulling out guns and making sure they were loaded. I did the same and tried to find a way to sneak up to the house.

"We're going in unprotected," Conor stated the obvious. "We go fast."

I nodded.

"Ready?" Conor asked. I didn't answer. Instead, I ran for the door, kicking it down with my foot. The lock had been flimsy and the door buckled immediately. Screams came from inside, forcing me into the house quickly, my gun raised as I entered every room. The house was quiet, I could barely hear anything now.

No shots had rung out which was a good thing as Conor and I split up to take the rooms separately. I cleared all the rooms except for the back of the house. We met up and Conor pointed through to the last room. We all looked toward the two sliding wooden doors that Amity was holed up in with Sloane.

I edged closer, lowering my gun. I knew Conor and Teeghan had my back but I was putting a lot of faith in the hope that Amity wouldn't kill me on sight or worse, kill Sloane.

I slid the doors open to see Amity holding a gun to Sloane's temple. Sloane was doing everything not to cry but I could see the terror in her eyes. It was killing me that it was because of me she was in this position. After all, she'd broken up with me because she didn't want any part of this life.

She was too pure of heart for this world.

And here I was, selfishly pulling her back into it just so I could be near her, to be able to smell that perfume that had my cock go crazy, to be able to see how her eyes glistened when she drank a cocktail that she had been thinking about all week.

Fuck.

Sloane was still very much on my fucking mind, turning me soft. My father hated what she did to me. Even after all these years, i could still hear his fucking voice in my head to end it with her. It was her or the family.

I'd made my choice the day she had broken my heart. Before I could tell her, she'd put an end to the Killian and Sloane show. Too hurt to tell her I'd chosen her, I'd let her break us apart.

Who knew what would have become of us if I'd run away with her that night, who knew what kind of person I would be now.

"Amity, please let Sloane go," I said. "Here, I'm putting my gun away."

Sloane stiffened when I put my gun in its holster. Amity kept her eyes on me and then on Conor who was edging in behind me.

"Get rid of them," Amity yelled. She was slowly losing control of the situation, which meant this was fucking dangerous for Sloane. We probably startled her, not real- izing we would figure out where she is so quickly.

"That's not going to happen," I told her. "We can talk, Amity, just you and me, yeah? Let Sloane go and I'll stay."

Sloane made a move to shake her head but Amity slammed the laxxing gun back to her temple. Sloane's lip trembled as she tried to hold her panic in.

"They go."

I turned to Conor and Teeghan. They wouldn't leave and I knew it.

"They won't go until you let Sloane go, but we can still talk."

Amity was losing her control and she knew it. I was slowly moving in closer to her and she was seeing that, tightening her grip on Sloane.

"Amity, is this about your husband?" Teeghan yelled out.

Amity's gaze switched to her. I saw Conor move in front of her instantly, protecting her, just as I wanted to do with Sloane.

One shot and I could take Amity out, but if her trigger finger was pushing down on the trigger, it could go off with the shot and kill Sloane too.

"What do you want?" I asked her, hoping she would focus back on me. I knew her. I'd known her since we were kids in school, surely I could reason with her.

"She wants...you," Sloane grunted.

I could barely process what had been said before I saw Amity release Sloane to smack her in the head with the butt of the gun. I saw Amity aim her gun to shoot at Sloane. I pulled my gun free and shot at her hand. Amity dropped the gun and yelped, looking down at her hand. Blood fell freely from her wound. I reached out and grabbed Sloane to pull her behind me. Conor and Teeghan took her and left the house. I ran after Amity as she scrambled to the window but for some reason, when I had the shot, I didn't take it.

Had the assassin in me become soft with age? There was I time, and not so long ago, when I would have gladly taken that shot and without question.

Before I could stop her, she ran for a large window to the side of the room. Pulling my gun back out, I shot at the frame but she was already out by the time I got to it. When I looked down, she was running. I ran to the back door to make chase but by the time I got there, she was gone. There was a patch of forest behind her house which she had disappeared into.

We got Sloane.

That was all that mattered...for now.

I put my gun in its holster and headed out to make sure Sloane was okay.

CHAPTER SIX

SLOANE

I took the cup of tea from Killian gratefully and huddled under the blanket near the fireplace. He sat down on the opposite chair. Since he had rescued me from Amity, he hadn't said a word. Instead, I had stayed in the back of the car with Teeghan who had let me sleep on her lap and he'd driven us back to town, back to the estate because I didn't want to go back to the cottage.

Now, it was just me and him. Teeghan and Conor had left an hour ago and yet Killian had been calm enough to let me breathe.

Still now, instead of rushing to ask me what had happened, he was sitting there, probably chewing himself out for not protecting me better.

"She's in love with you," I told him, sipping at the tea. It was warming me up on this unseasonably cold night. I couldn't tell if I was shaking from the shock of having a gun at my temple or the chill in the air. "Amity."

"I'm no angel, you fucking know that, and I've done shit

that I don't want you to know about. I probably shouldn't have gotten involved with Amity, especially considering her marital status with one of my brothers' men."

It hurt to think of him sleeping with her, knowing my history with her in school, but I'd been the one to walk away from Killian. I knew I had no right to be upset about it.

"She loved you before I came to town. She said she had been trying to get you to notice for years before I came here and you and I fell in love. I should have seen it earlier. The first time we had sex, she was so upset with me and that was when our friendship died out."

"All this time?" he asked. "I never looked at her like someone I wanted to date. Hell, I didn't want to date at all and then you blew into my life and that's all I wanted."

I felt oddly vindicated by that comment.

"Was she really married?"

Killian nodded. "Yeah, he was killed in a shootout. He worked for Conor."

"But she never loved him?"

"I don't know but she cheated on him a fair bit."

"I think she always loved you, Kill. She didn't want to kill me but I think she would have if you didn't pick her."

Killian sighed and looked over at the fire that was mesmerizing.

"I'm sorry you got caught up in this."

I didn't know what to say but I could feel the pain in his voice and that hurt me. It wasn't his fault that I was friends with Teeghan. She had happily adopted the O'Farrell way of life and she was happy.

"I won't lie, Kill, it was scary but something inside of me knew you'd save me."

He smirked, but didn't meet my gaze again. Killian had deep thoughts, scary thoughts and he would zone out like this to spare me having to know what he was thinking. It was both annoying and scary, but I knew I didn't want to know what was flashing through his dark mind.

"I'll head back to the cottage tomorrow morning," I told him.

Finally, he looked back at me. "You don't need to. You can stay as long as you want. I'll be going to London tomorrow for a few days. You can relax here and do what you want. Lorcan can find you someone to look out for you if you need to go to the city or you need to travel. I doubt Amity will try again but she got away and she'll be mad she didn't win."

I felt a little down trodden at the thought of him leaving but I knew I shouldn't be. I was falling back in love with him, and I knew it.

"I still have to pack up the rest of my boxes and organize to get them shipped to Dublin. My cousin offered me a job there."

Killian looked away again for a moment, and I waited with bated breath to hear if he would tell me to stay. Some part of me wanted him to do that, and another wanted him to ignore it. If we fought, I could walk away from him, hating him and hopefully make a life in Dublin.

"That's good," he said. "You should go."

The pain that shot out of my chest was brutal, and I felt my body shaking with emotion. Killian stood up, and looked down at me for a brief moment.

I was unable to read his emotions. This was the assassin.

This was the Killian that his father would have wanted all along.

This wasn't my Killian.

"You'll be happier there."

He left the room, and me, quickly. Tears poured out

over my cheeks quickly as I struggled to put my tea down on the table before I dropped it. I collapsed onto the ground, sucking in deep breaths to try and calm my body down. I couldn't tell if it was the rejection from Killian or the fact I'd almost died today, maybe both, but I was not okay.

————

TEEGHAN'S CAR pulled up outside the cottage just as I was about to book the removalist. I knew she wouldn't let me stay here alone, not after everything that had happened yesterday. As much as I had wanted to stay at the estate, it just felt so horrible without Killian.

"Hey girl," she announced as she came in with a box of wine and a bag of what I could only assume was a wide array of snack food.

"How much do you think I can drink?" I asked her.

"Bitch, this is for both of us. Don't get all greedy on me."

I rolled my eyes as she put the wine in the fridge and fiddled around in the kitchen.

"I packed all of my plates already," I called out to her. She poked her head out of the kitchen and held up a couple of plastic plates.

"As if I didn't already think about that," she replied. "Come on, girl."

I chuckled as I locked in the removalists for tomorrow morning. My cousin had already booked a storage room for the boxes in Dublin and my life would soon start.

"I'm going to miss the hell out of you," Teeghan said as she came into the room with a platter of cheeses, fruit, and hummus. She put it down on the table and went back to the kitchen for another platter of different biscuits and crackers.

"Who am I going to take out for cocktails when Conor is being annoying?"

"I hear your friendship with Lorcan has been the talk in that estate."

Teeghan sat down, rolling her eyes. "Those boys need to get a hobby and leave the gossiping to us girls."

"I'm scared of the hobby they would take up if they had time."

Teeghan didn't laugh. Instead, she grabbed a cracker and dipped it in the hummus. "You know I hardly know what's going on with their businesses. Conor keeps me well protected. It's not as scary as you think."

"Tee, you've always been different. I don't like the intimidation, the criminal roots of that family. I just don't want to be around darkness."

Teeghan finished her cracker and sat back in the chair. "Darkness? I guess it's how you look at it. They have kept this town from going down a rabbit hole like every other city or town that is full of crime. We are relatively safe here, trust me."

"It doesn't matter anyway," I said. "Killian isn't interested in a relationship. He wants me gone just as much as I need to get away from this place."

"I doubt that's what he wants."

"Teeghan. We weren't going to get back together and have our second chance romance," I said, a little frustrated that we were still talking about this. "I am his past just as he is mine. Dublin is my future."

Teeghan waited for the longest of moments with that dead gaze that scared so many before she snapped out of it and shrugged her shoulders before she grabbed a grape from the platter. "If that's what you wish, then it's what you shall have."

"One more night of no talk about men, and especially no talk about the O'Farrell's."

"You got it, babe."

Teeghan got up and moved over to her bag and pulled out a portable speaker. She hooked up her phone and started to blast songs from our younger years.

I finalized my removalist and put my laptop to the side.

One more night of fun before I started to heal in Dublin.

KILLIAN

"THIS IS THE PLACE, BOSS," Jimmy said as we sat in the car outside a club. I hated coming to London, even more so when I didn't know who the enemy was but I needed to get away from the estate and away from Sloane as she left for Dublin. I couldn't risk stopping her from leaving. I'd already gotten her into enough shit as it was and Amity was just the tip of the fucking iceberg. I knew Ronan was still out there, looking for blood. Sloane had made the right decision that day when she walked away from me, from us.

"Let's go," I announced as I got out of the car. Liam and Jimmy both stood behind me, my backup if needed. I had no intention of needing help tonight though. This was a fact finding mission. Lorcan was keeping an eye on things back home, and Conor was helping with my business while I was gone. I didn't intend on being gone for long but there were always those odd occasions when you got blindsided.

We headed inside, the door guy allowing us entry quickly.

"Heads up," I said to the boys. "Whoever it is, knows we're here."

We headed to the bar once we got inside and finally got to the front after a few minutes. The bartender was overworked but seemed nice enough.

"Who runs this place?" I asked him.

He looked toward a camera briefly before he threw his towel over his shoulder. A sign to his bosses that someone was asking about them, I assumed. It was the same thing my bartenders did at my own club.

"You looking for him for any particular reason?"

"Just needed to talk to him about a few mercs he sent my way."

He was suspicious of me, which was fine, but I didn't intend to tell a bartender my plans. He nodded toward a booth at the back after a short pause, probably seeing if I would eventually divulge our plans.

I was no fucking rookie.

"Go sit over there, he'll be with you shortly."

I nodded and took my boys over to it. The bartender came over not long after and put a bottle of whiskey down on the table with four glasses.

"I don't like this," Liam said. "He's pouring Jameson. He knows who we are already."

I didn't want to voice it but I was having the same issue with this whole thing. Who the fuck were we working with here?

It didn't take long before we were joined by a man, and not someone I would have expected to run a fucking huge operation that could hurt us.

"Gentlemen," he said, taking a seat and pouring our drinks. "Nice of you to come all the way to London to speak."

"Cut the crap, who are you?" I yelled over the music.

The blond haired, blue eyed mama's boy in front of me

had the audacity to smirk as he took a sip of the Jameson in his glass. "I'm not who you think I am. In fact, you'll never get close enough to who it is that's going to take over your business. I'm a cog in a very big machine."

"The man asked who you were," Liam said, his rich accent coming through. "Answer him."

"Lawrence Somers. I run this side of London."

"And why are you here and not the man I need to speak with?"

"I'm guessing you were led here for a reason and that's probably because all of our businesses are connected to him."

I was getting tired of the run around. "This guy doesn't know anything."

Liam and I pushed out of the booth but before we could go, I felt someone behind us. Turning, I saw the fist only moments before it hit me in the side of the head and the world turned upside down.

———

THE ROOM I was in when I came to was dimly lit, just one lightbulb hanging on a long cord from the ceiling like every bad interrogation movie out there. The side of my head ached and my body was stiff. I wondered how long I had been here.

I took in the room, Liam and Jimmy were nowhere to be seen, nor was anyone else. I was tied to a chair, and the ropes were pretty tight. Any movement caused a sharp friction over the skin of my wrists.

I was about to call out when the door opened and the same blond haired fucker from before stepped inside.

"Oh good, you're awake. I was starting to think I was going to need to torture you awake."

"You have no idea the wrath that's going to beat down your door if you don't release us."

"I wouldn't worry so much," Lawrence said. "Your men are gone and I know you told your brothers you would be gone for a few days so we have that at least."

My rage mounted. I knew what he meant by my men were gone. It would be the same thing I would do if I were in his position. I'd worked with Liam and Jimmy for years now. Never did I think I'd come here and lose my men.

"What do you want with me?"

"Nothing, really. I didn't even know you were an issue until recently."

"Who the fuck do you work for?" I asked through grit teeth.

"I'm pretty sure you know I'm not going to tell you. Look, I don't want to keep torturing you. You're going to lose your family empire, I feel like that's bad enough. You just need to stay here until we can lure your brothers out here."

I could only imagine what they had planned for us but what they didn't know was we had a long standing tradition that there was always one O'Farrell in Ireland. They'd never get what they wanted.

That's when it hit me.

How did he know my brothers thought I would be gone for days? The only way he could know that is if either Jimmy or Liam told him or if we had a mole in our house. I knew Jimmy and Liam wouldn't say shit, especially if they knew they would die, so that meant my brothers were in danger and I had no way of letting them know.

Fuck.

CHAPTER SEVEN

KILLIAN

The fist came toward my cheek again, this time though my face moved to the side. Blood was dripping down into my eyes with every movement. This fucker had been working me over for the past thirty minutes. I didn't know how long I had been here but it had to be days by now. My brothers would be suspicious I hadn't returned and probably would come down here.

That's the last thing that needed to happen. If they had all three of us, Ireland could be easily taken. It was a long standing tradition that Ireland was never without an O'Farrell. I could only hope one of them stayed behind.

"You are a tough bugger, aren't ya?" the guy who had been torturing me for the past day or so said. He had a rich Manchurian accent and I could tell he wasn't too bright. Lawrence hadn't been around, so I could only assume he was conducting business while he had me hostage.

That just fucking annoyed me.

"Come on, mate," he said, punching me in the ribs

again. At least a couple of them had to be broken by now but I wasn't going to let this fucker know. "Give me something to give those fuckers."

I sat myself back up on the chair, the ropes tying my hands behind me were rubbing into my skin. I could feel the burn of the rope in my opened wounds.

"Shit, wish you were on our side," he said before he left the room. I hissed as I breathed, knowing he was gone. The pain from my ribs was intense, and my breathing was shallow. If I didn't get help soon, I knew I was a goner.

A loud sound thundered through the room from outside. Men were shouting, shots were ringing out. I tried to rub my ropes loose but it was only causing even more pain.

It took what felt like a lifetime before the door was opened. In burst Callum, one of Conor's men. He ran for me, putting his gun down on the ground before he cut my ropes loose. I slumped on the chair, pulling my aching arms into my lap.

"I'm dust," I said to him. It amazed me how weak I sounded.

"I've got you."

He grabbed his gun and handed it to me before he wrapped one of my arms around his neck. I could feel my ribs pulling with the movement but it was the only way I was getting out of here. My little brother had come to save the day.

I was never going to live this down.

Callum grabbed his other gun and shot at anyone who moved in front of us. As he dragged me out of the hell hole I had been in. Callum leaned me up against a wall close to the door and ran back to grab something. I was righting myself when I saw through the window that some were fleeing.

I hobbled over to the window and opened it just as I saw a familiar face getting into a car.

Fucking Ronan O'Brien.

No fucking shit. I pulled my arm up and armed the gun, taking a shot at the door he was holding. He dodged it and got in the car as it was taking off down the street.

Fuck.

If my ribs and arms weren't in so much pain, I would have made that shot and our troubles would be over.

Conor ran to my side and helped me out to the car.

"You good?" he asked me, looking down at me as I sat in the backseat.

"Yeah, get me home."

Conor nodded and I felt the darkness of sleep take me as I laid down.

———

DAYS LATER

A knock on the door startled me awake and I grabbed my gun on my nightstand. Slowly the door opened and I saw Teeghan's red hair poke around the corner.

"Just me."

I lowered the gun and edged up on the bed, holding my aching ribs in the process.

"Don't exert yourself," she said. "I come bearing gifts."

She handed me a bottle of whiskey.

I smirked over at her and took it gratefully. "Don't think the doc wants me to drink this."

"What he doesn't know, can't hurt him."

I cracked the bottle open and took a big swig. The

amber liquid burned as it went down my throat. Ahhh, I was home.

"How did Conor know?"

"The idiots who took you sent Liam and Jimmy's bloodied bodies back to us with a note. We traced it to the place they had you."

"It wasn't an accident. They wanted you to find me. They knew I wouldn't crack and if they killed me, then they would face the wrath of Lorcan and Conor."

Teeghan nodded. "They were mad as hell. I've never seen them fly off the rails like that."

"We would do anything for any of our brothers. We just don't talk about it."

Teeghan smiled before a low rumble of a laugh bubbled out. "Yeah, I get it, you're manly men."

I couldn't roll my eyes enough at her jab. "Where are they now?"

"Working out who the fuck had the balls to torture their brother."

I didn't want to tell her what I found out. I wanted to tell Lorcan. He would know the best way to go about it.

"Why are you really here?" I asked her, knowing her a little too well to know she wouldn't come and give me whiskey while I was resting without a good reason.

"Damn it," she replied. "I thought I was playing it cool."

"If this is about Sloane-"

"Of course it's about Sloane."

"Look, Tee. I know you love her and you want her around but it's safer for her to be gone. People know I care about her and people want to hurt me. I can't risk that."

Teeghan sat up on the end of the bed and looked down at the floor for a few moments. I thought maybe she had accepted it but she got off the bed and looked down at me.

There was a coldness in her gaze that should have scared me.

"Did you ever think that maybe she had a right to make that decision for herself?"

"She did, Teeghan. All those years ago, she broke up with me because she didn't want to be a part of the O'Farrell way of life."

Teeghan moved around the room, as if she were burning off steam. "You are such an idiot. Why the fuck are men such idiots when it comes to women?"

"Maybe because we're not women?" I countered, realizing it would probably annoy her more and I was injured. If she wanted to take a swing, I'd go down easily.

She turned on me, that same darkness in her eyes that made me curious about how someone as sweet as her could look so menacing in a split second. "She was fucking eighteen. She didn't know what she wanted and all she had seen were the women in your lives being killed or maimed. She was scared because she didn't want you to turn into your daddy."

I'd been scared of doing that too. Unfortunately, I was very much like him. Lorcan and I both were in our own ways.

"She's fucking miserable in Dublin, by the way."

Teeghan moved toward the door.

"She's only just moved there. She deserves to be happy, doesn't she?"

Teeghan just shook her head as she opened the door. Pausing before she moved through it, she looked back. "Maybe, so do you, fuckhead."

She was gone before I could throw her words back at her. We had bigger fish to fry than my non-existent love life.

Telling Sloane to leave was the hardest thing I could have done.

But it was better off this way.

Eventually, I would start to believe that and we could both move on.

For now, I had a fucker to kill and a business to run.

SLOANE

"THAT'S THE LAST OF THEM," I heard my cousin's husband, Darren, say as he hefted the box into the apartment I'd rented for the next three months. It was a run down place but it would get me through the next stage of my life.

"Thanks, Darren. I'll get in touch with Sinead tomorrow about work."

He nodded and headed back to his car. He'd never been one for words, especially, not with a cousin of his wife that he barely knew. When he drove off, I closed the door and looked around at all my boxes. This was going to take me hours to unpack.

Then again, I was only going to move again. Was it even worth unpacking?

I moved into the kitchen to look through the boxes in there when I saw the hamper on the kitchen counter. I grabbed the card and saw the words written there, making my heart thunder in my chest.

Slo,

I hate that you left me here alone but I get what you need to do.

Come back soon, you hear.

I put some vitals in this hamper for you.

Tee x

I put the card down and opened the cellophane to reveal a hamper full of chocolates, candy, magazines and then behind that, I saw the vibrator and lube. I rolled my eyes and felt the chuckle bubble to the surface. I was going to miss that girl. I'd not had the heart to tell her I had no intention of returning. I was probably going to head down south to Killarney and set up there. My mother's aunt had property down there and I remembered it fondly. It was far enough away that the O'Farrell's wouldn't be mentioned constantly and I wouldn't be reminded of the fierce attraction to Killian. Sure, it would take a while to get him out of my head, but no doubt I could find myself a nice Irishman who could take away all my pain. I might even think about children one day.

I grabbed the box of chocolates and headed into my bedroom. Darren had made sure my bed was set up and the TV was hooked up already. He was a fucking gem. He was exactly the kind of guy I needed to find down in Killarney.

One who had never touched a gun in his life.

A safe guy.

Flicking the TV on, I chucked the chocolates on the bedside table and turned my lamp on before I went about making the bed. Since I was a kid, I hated to make the bed. The sheet never wanted to fit properly. As I pulled myself across the bed to get the other side tucked in, I heard a familiar name on the TV.

Turning over, I looked up at the photo of Killian on the news. Turning the TV up, I sat and watched what they considered breaking news.

"Feared and admired by many, the middle son of the monster Finneas O'Farrell, was caught in some trouble recently and it appears it's spread throughout Ireland and into England. He's been admitted to hospital with multiple broken bones and a punctured lung after dueling with some English criminals. What brought him to England is a mystery but sources say he's been getting in with the Reyes Cartel, and bringing it to Dublin."

I turned the channel so I didn't have to hear anymore. I couldn't even get away from him here. I knew the O'Farrell's pretty much ran all of central Ireland, and technically they ran southern Ireland too but most hadn't heard of the brothers down south, but for him to be on the news like this in Dublin...it had to be big news. Someone was putting him on blast.

Killian was in trouble and the first thing I wanted to do was run back and make sure he was okay.

Fuck, Sloane, you've gone and fallen in love with him again, haven't you?

I changed the TV to a movie and got under my blankets, grabbing my box of chocolates. I tried to rid the thought of a badly injured Killian from my mind but I knew it was useless. Perhaps after a good night's sleep, I could refocus on myself rather than thinking about him. We broke up for a reason, I just had to remember why.

KILLIAN

LORCAN GOT out of the car first, followed by Conor and me. I was still in pain from last week but the doc said I was healing well. The news report on me was fake, probably planted by Ronan and his cronies. I couldn't believe he'd hidden from sight again and was unable to be located even with our extensive contacts searching for him. How the fuck could he possibly be able to escape from us?

His brother Jeremiah had been hiding out in one of our old properties nobody knew about for months now. He'd been slowly giving us information on his brother and what he'd been planning for years. Who knew the fucker had it in him to betray his own blood?

We headed inside to find Jeremiah passed out asleep with two whores laying over him, stark naked. Lorcan kicked his hand, jolting him awake.

The women cracked their eyes open and scattered to a bedroom somewhere. It wasn't exactly a sight you'd want to wake up to, having the three O'Farrell brothers standing over you.

"When we said you could stay here, O'Brien, we didn't mean you could turn it into a drug and sex pen."

Jeremiah sat up, rubbing his eyes as if we'd inconvenienced him. He was lucky he still had fingers to rub the sleep out of his eyes. Lorcan sure had softened in his old age.

"Get some clothes on," Conor said. "Meet us outside."

We headed out the back and sat down at the table out there. This place had been built by our uncle who had hated the criminal world. Instead, he had tended to injured men and helped to hide people who needed the sanctuary.

When he died, he'd gifted it to Lorcan but he'd never give up city life to move out here.

So it had become a safe house.

Jeremiah appeared at the table a few moments later, dressed and looking a little less sleepy.

"Sit down."

He did and looked at each of us with determination and a little fear. He knew this wasn't good.

"You found my brother."

"Yeah," I said. "Rather, he found me. In London."

"He has contacts there, I've told you about them," he defended himself.

"He's running something big down there. How connected is he?" I asked him. Jeremiah looked at my cut lip and my black eye and it dawned on him. His brother had gotten the best of me. I hated to admit it, but it hurt my pride a little. No one got the best of me. Everyone knew that. It was the reason I hadn't shown myself in the club too. I didn't want people to think they could best me and get away with it. But that was precisely what Ronan had done.

"He has a few contacts but I was never involved with that side. He wanted me to run things from dad's shop, keep an ear to the ground so to speak."

"Who do you know he trusts?" Conor asked.

"I guess you could speak with Darren Lewis."

"Darren?"

"Yeah, he's some rich suit he connected with when he first dreamed of taking over the town. He lives in Dublin now with his wife, but he still runs a lot of things from there."

Darren...why did that name sound familiar to me? I couldn't put my finger on it but it didn't feel good. Something was up with this Darren guy and I needed to find out.

I got up and pulled my phone from my pocket, moving away from them to call Teeghan.

"Hey," she answered. "Are you guys almost done? I'm thinking of getting lunch delivered."

"Don't let Walter hear you say that," I told her. "That's not why I'm calling anyway."

"What's up?"

"Does the name Darren Lewis mean anything to you?"

She was hesitant for a moment, and I felt my gut drop. This wasn't going to be something I wanted to hear, and I knew instantly it was about Sloane.

"Well, yeah, but why?"

"Who is he?" I demanded.

"He's married to Sinead Carpenter," she said. My stomach plummeted and I felt bile rise in my throat.

"You mean Sloane's cousin Sinead?"

"Yep, the one she's working with down in Dublin. Why do you ask?"

I hung up the phone and walked back over to the table. "We gotta go."

Lorcan and Conor didn't question me, they simply followed me out to the car. I got in behind the wheel and took off, leaving a cloud of smoke in our wake.

"What is it?" Lorcan asked, holding onto his door as I raced through the streets to get back home.

"Sloane's in trouble again."

"Jesus," Conor swore. "How the hell can one little woman get into so much strife?"

"Tell me."

I turned to Lorcan briefly before I refocused on the road. "Darren is her cousin's husband. She just moved closer to him."

"Gun it to Dublin," Conor said. "We need to find out more about this fucker though. Call in the recruits, Lor."

Lorcan was already hitting the button on his phone to call his men to look into Darren Lewis and Sinead Carpenter. My heart was in my throat, making it hard to breathe. I thought letting her go was the best choice but it turns out, it was probably the worst. I'd let her into the enemy's hands, again, and all because I thought being around her was too hard.

Man the fuck up, Kill.

CHAPTER EIGHT

SLOANE

"This is your desk," Sinead said as she wheeled us around a partition to a small desk with a computer, keyboard and mouse on it. "I'll come by with your password in a minute and get you set up."

"Thanks," I said as she walked away. Being in an office again was strange. I'd worked in one for my uncle when I just married Sean but had hated the hours. I'd worked in shops since, but having moved over here, I needed something a little more substantial to get me through finding my own place. I had moved into an apartment owned by my aunt so I hadn't had to pay exorbitant rents while I was home. This was a whole new ball game.

As scary as that was.

I had to do it.

I sat down at the desk and ran my hands over the clean desk, and the keyboard to get a feel for the keys.

I could do this.

Sinead came back and handed me a few folders.

"These are the guides and manuals for the software you'll be using. Every answer is in here if you can't find me. I'll be in and out of meetings all day today so just flick through it."

She handed me a piece of paper with a username and password on it.

"This is just your login, once you log in, it will pop up with a box to change your password."

I nodded, taking it all in, and trying not to be overwhelmed.

"Once you do that, your programs will load. The outlook icon is the one with the envelope. Click on it. It will open and you can start to click into your emails. You will have one with a welcome message, and the other three are induction links so you can do them today. They will probably take all morning but it's a requirement. Once you're done, just send me an email and I will come over to give you some stuff."

I nodded, unable to form words at how fast she was talking. Business Sinead was not like cousin Sinead at all. It's amazing how some people could completely change when they were at work. Not me. I was the same old Sloane anytime you saw me.

Sinead moved off with her assistant and I started to login. It was as easy as she said and I soon clicked into my email. The welcome email from HR was standard and a simple template they sent off every time someone started. The second email was the first induction link I needed to start.

Once I clicked into that, I tried not to fall asleep as the man with a monotone spoke about the company I now worked for. A coffee free morning was not a good idea.

———

THE CAFE WAS BRIMMING when I finally got a chance to get over here. It was just across the street from the office and it looked like it was a popular choice. I stood in line and mentally changed my order at least six times. Who knew what I'd order when I got up to the counter.

Once I progressed, a bright eyed brunette looked over at me with a smile. "What can we get you?"

"Uh a Turkey BLAT."

Shit.

She smiled. "A BLAT or a Turkey Sub? Or both?"

"I'm sorry, a Turkey Sub."

"Any drinks?"

"No, thanks."

She gave me a ticket and I stepped to the side. As I looked down at the number, and the people milling in the collect area, I knew it was going to be a long wait. I headed outside to get some fresh air only to be assaulted with plumes of smoke from the smokers. I moved to the other side and sat at the end of the bench and looked down at my phone.

I saw the message from Teeghan and smiled as I opened it. When I read what she had asked me, I frowned.

TEE

Why would Killian be asking about Darren?

SLOANE

I've no idea. He shouldn't know his name at all. I've never told him.

TEE

He didn't answer me when I asked and now none of the brothers are calling me back. Could be nothing. You know Killian.

SADLY, I did. And I knew that if none of them were answering their phone, it wasn't good. Why the hell would he be asking about Darren?

My number was called a few moments later and I quickly ran inside and grabbed my order before I hightailed it back over the street to work. I sat down on a table near the kitchen and ate my sub. I marveled at how good it was. The bread was fresh and the cranberry sauce was to die for. I had to stop myself from moaning from delight.

Sinead had been gone all day, but I'd managed to learn quite a bit already. This job was going to be a breeze.

I finished up and decided to go for a walk around the building before I went back to the desk. As I walked around, I heard an odd sound from another building. As I cautiously continued on my path, I caught sight of a man with his pants down as he was ramming into a woman bent over and leaning against the wall. I gasped and hid behind a bush as I noticed the woman was someone I knew.

I was watching my cousin hold onto the brick wall as someone I knew to be her boss was fucking her from behind. He was going hard at it while she looked quite bored.

What the fuck?

I quickly moved away, and went back to the office but the image of her cheating on her husband was emblazoned in my retinas.

Sinead and Darren seemed to really love each other, from what I had seen.

Nothing was ever as it seemed.

KILLIAN

CONOR GOT out of the car and headed into the gas station to pay. I was impatient, losing my mind that she was in danger again. I shouldn't have pushed her away. I couldn't protect her in Dublin.

"She's fine," Lorcan said, from beside me. "If they wanted to use her against you, we would have heard something. It's a long con, I guarantee you."

"If Ronan is involved, I know he's going to grab her and hold her. If he even touches her, Lor, I will end his entire fucking existence."

I meant it too. The rage inside of me was overwhelming. I hated fuckers, but I'd never hated anyone more than Ronan O'Brien. If he thought he was going to use Sloane, he had another thing coming.

This has to end. And it had to end now.

Conor finally got back to the car and I took off as fast as I could. As I drove toward Dublin, I couldn't help but remember all the times Sloane had been annoyed when I would show up where she was, even though we were dating, she knew it was because I was being overprotective.

She hated it then, and I knew she was going to hate it now but I couldn't risk losing her.

She was standing in line, laughing and enjoying time with Amity and some other friends I recognised from school.

We'd fought the night before and I couldn't get it out of my head. I hated it when she was angry with me, but she'd brought up my dad again and I couldn't get into that with her.

I was about to walk away when I noticed the guy come up to them. Sloane didn't know him, I could tell by the surprise on her face that she didn't know him nor had she been expecting him. My hackles were rising, I could feel the heat in my face and neck as my fists balled next to me. Who the fuck was this guy?

Amity was flirting with him as he smiled at the girls and said something to make them laugh. He was aiming his attention at Sloane though. I could see the way he was undressing her with his eyes.

He had a fucking deathwish.

Everyone knew Sloane was mine.

The only thing that wasn't pushing me over to them to kick the shit out of this guy was the fact Sloane needed me to trust her. She needed to know I wasn't going to beat anyone just for looking.

But fuck me, I wanted to. I wanted to lock her in a room forever and her and me would live our lives fucking and eating takeout.

I knew that was impossible, there was no way we could sustain ourselves and there was no way I could get away from my dad.

It was inevitable I would be recruited to work for him in the next few months, once I hit eighteen. That was why Sloane and I had been fighting so much. She could sense it too.

The guy was talking to Sloane now. I could see she was answering him politely but she didn't want to be. Amity was still trying to get his attention but he only had eyes for

Sloane. I couldn't blame him. She had hooked me the second I saw her too, but she was my girl. He had no right to be talking to her, and if she didn't want it, she sure as hell shouldn't be put in that position. I was about to go over there when I saw him leave. Amity and the girls were fawning over him but Sloane couldn't be bothered with joining them.

My girl.

I turned to leave and get back to the estate before my father blew a gasket but something gnawed at me. I felt like I needed to stay. My mother had always told me never to ignore intuition and she'd always been right. I plonked myself down at the tables in the food court, across from the cinema. Families and other kids my age had gotten up and left the surrounding tables. They knew who I was here. It was hard to hide being Finneas O'Farrell's son. It used to bother me but it worked in my favor from time to time too.

The wait was excruciating, and I knew that movie was going to go for hours but I wasn't going to second guess myself here. I had to make sure she was okay.

I got up from my seat and moved over to the counter for the burger place but before I could get in line, I saw movement from the cinema in a reflective surface. I turned around to see Amity and Sloane fighting. Sloane was shoving her away as Amity tried to drag her back inside.

What the hell?

Sloane clearly didn't want to be in there but Amity was almost forcing her back inside. I started to make a move toward them to break it up when I saw the fucker from before coming out of the cinema toward them with a cocky grin on his face.

The fury returned and I felt something inside of me boil up and push me toward them at a furious pace. Amity saw me first and backed up, her eyes wide with horror as she tried to get away from what she knew was going to happen.

The fucker had his hands on Sloane's arm, and he was trying to pull her toward him. She was pushing him back, and then her eyes flicked to me right before she urged him to go. He turned around just as I got to him. Instantly he let go of her arm and tried to put his arms up to stop me but it was going to take more than that. I slugged him hard across the jaw, his head snapped to the side, blood spraying across the white tiles. He fell to his knees and then to his ass as he tried to pull himself away from me. I got down and started to pummel him with my fist. His teeth catching on the skin of my knuckles and ripping. The blood coming from his mouth and nose was extreme, his eye was closed and he was gasping for air as I felt arms on me, trying to pull me off.

I shoved at the security who were trying to break it up and they all fell to their asses on the tiled floor.

That's when I heard her.

"Killian, stop it."

I turned around, my fist hovering just inches from his very broken nose, and looked at her. She had tears in her eyes as she pleaded with me to leave with her.

"Please, Killian, let's go."

She took my bloodied hand and helped me to my feet. I wrapped my arm around her shoulders and she led me out of the complex. The sound of sirens erupted around us as the cops headed our way.

"You need to go."

I opened the car door and got in but she wasn't moving. She looked angry, and a little sad.

"Slo."

"No," she said. "I can't even go to the movies without you stalking me, Kill. Don't you see how creepy that is?"

She was right. I knew she'd be angry but I knew in my gut she would need me today. How did I explain that to her?

"Sloane, we can talk about this later. Get in the goddamn car."

"No, you can't tell me what to do. I can't do this right now. Killian, you need to go."

"Not without you."

She was looking nervously at the cops approaching and then at me. She knew what would happen if they got me into their car. Finneas would lose his shit and the town would suffer. Probably those cops would lose their jobs, maybe their lives.

She groaned and ran for the passenger seat and I tore out of the car park, toward the estate. One of the fuckers decided to chase me. I loved the thrill that shot down my spine as I tore through the streets and toward the estate.

Sloane was gripping the sides of her seat as I maneuvered around tight corners until I got onto the road that would lead to the estate. The cop was right behind me. Probably a rookie wanting to make the bust. They all knew that if they busted one of us out in the streets doing something illegal, we were fair game. Once I got onto the estate grounds, they couldn't fucking touch me.

I put the pedal to the metal as I tore past the wrought iron O'Farrell gates and down the long drive. The cop stopped just outside of the gates, knowing full well what would happen to him if he crossed the line. I smirked at that and pulled up outside the doors. Sloane hadn't said a word to me since she got in the car and now she was staring straight ahead.

"Come inside, clean up," I told her. She finally looked down at her shirt and saw the blood stains.

"Fine," she said, coldly. "But I'm calling for a ride. We seriously need to talk about boundaries, Killian."

"I know."

"I mean it. I can't be your Rapunzel."

I had no idea what the fuck that meant but I nodded and watched as he got out of the car and headed inside. I tried to hide the smile, knowing I'd won some kind of battle today, but there would be a time when enough was enough.

SLOANE

I turned the key into the lock and opened my apartment. It was dark outside now, after being forced to go for drinks after with Darren and Sinead, and pretend I hadn't seen Sinead giving it up for her boss just hours earlier. It had been exhausting. I threw my bag down and turned on the lights only to gasp and stumble backward when I saw who was sitting on my recliner.

"Killian."

He stood up, a grave look on his face. "Hi, Sloane."

"What the fuck are you doing in my apartment?" I shot at him, anger replacing my exhaustion very quickly.

"I'm not here to start shit...I just need to tell you something."

"And you couldn't pick up a phone?"

"In hindsight, that was an option but moreover, I didn't think you hated me this much."

I could see the pain on his face, and I knew I was already in a mood, mainly because I'd had a big day and was exhausted but mostly because he was the one who wanted me to move away, he's the one who didn't want me around and yet here he was...a week later, breaking into my apartment and now he apparently had something so important to tell me he couldn't pick up a phone.

"You told me to fuck off and go to Dublin, that it was best for me to move on. Now, you're here, not a week after I leave? What kind of game is this?"

"No game," he said quickly. "Look, Sloane, you know I don't play this emotion shit well. I never did. I told you to come here, away from me, because I thought you'd be safe but turns out, my judgment is off. I don't know why you'd be so mad. You're the one who didn't want to be part of my life all those years ago. I'm just trying to respect those wishes."

I felt like slapping him. How the fuck could he think he could take the high road right now?

"Are you fucking kidding me, Kill?" I started to walk toward him. "I broke up with you because you were turning into your father. I spent years getting over you, truthfully, I was never over you. I was pretending to be okay that you chose crime over me but I hated you for that. I hated that I was never good enough for you to just be the Killian I fell in love with."

"That's not who I am, Sloane, and you know it. You wanted me to be something I wasn't and I couldn't do that for you. I am who I am. You either take me as I am or you walk away, once and for all."

"You're making it pretty fucking hard to do that," I shot back at him.

He shook his head, defeated.

"Fine," he said as he started to walk away. I grabbed his wrist to stop him. I wasn't done with this. But before I could get my words out, he had spun us around, my back against the wall and his face right up against mine. I could feel his breath on me, my heart hammering in my chest at just how furious he looked. His eyes were dark and intimidating. That's when I realized, I had the calm assassin staring into my eyes like he wanted to take me out.

His eyes flicked to my lips, which I had wet just moments ago. Before I could think about what I was going to do, his lips crushed against mine in a soul-stealing, hot kiss. I moaned into his mouth as his hands moved under my shirt, pulling it out of my skirt.

Whatever happened tomorrow I didn't care, because right now, I needed Killian in every way possible. A goodbye fuck was exactly what my body needed.

He moved his hands down over my ass and lifted me up higher against the wall. I wound my arms around his neck, running my fingers through those glossy black curls and pulling slightly. He grunted into my mouth, his tongue tangling with mine.

I wrapped my legs around his waist, realizing that I was already wet, feeling that familiar pooling in my panties whenever I was near him.

He didn't break from my lips as I felt him walk us toward my bedroom. I didn't know how long he'd been in my apartment before I got home but that was a fight we could have tomorrow.

He dropped me on the bed and peeled his shirt off. Seeing that heavily tattooed, and ripped chest did things to my insides that I couldn't control. Whether that made me incredibly conceited and shallow, I didn't care, but I did feel the need to run my nails over those hard ridges to hear his hiss. I lived for that hiss because I knew no one else could make him hiss. As he pulled the belt out from his jeans, I heard the loud thud as the buckle hit the floor. He came for me, his hands grabbing my skirt and yanking it down my legs, followed by my panties. I felt the cool night air touch my wet lips, instantly causing my hips to roll in excitement. His hand reached out and pulled me up by my shirt. I put my hands down behind me to hold myself up as he ripped the shirt apart, buttons flying all over the room. It took no time at all for him to rid me of my bra. Sitting completely naked on the bed, I looked over at him, still in jeans.

"Get 'em off, Kill."

He smirked as he unzipped and slid the jeans down. He was commando as usual, which did even more to me than his kiss.

Killian slowly got on his knees, in front of me, and grabbed my legs. Pulling me forward, I fell back on the bed, my ass on the very edge as he pulled my legs up and over his shoulders. His mouth was on my pussy before I could readjust myself into a comfortable position. I gave up as his tongue did things to me. He put one of his forearms over my hips and held me in place as he licked, nipped and sucked at my pussy and my clit. I screamed out, clutching at the sheet underneath me, pulling it up at the corners. I threw my head back into the mattress as he delivered sweet, sweet torture to my pussy. The nerves in my legs tingled with the onslaught of what I could only imagine was going to be an earth shattering climax. His tongue delved into me, sliding along one side of my labia and up to my clit. I knew better than to push away from him so I squeezed my thighs over his face as my clit pulsed. It didn't stop him though, as I writhed underneath him as my body tensed just moments before my clit exploded, my pussy throbbed as my hips rolled out what an orgasm that took my breath away.

I felt like I was about to melt into the mattress, my body completely at ease from the stress of the day. Killian sat back, a cocky grin on his face. One that usually had me weak at the knees but I didn't want to fall into this trap again.

Finding the strength to push myself up off the bed, I started to walk away. "I think you were about to leave."

All I heard next was a primal grunt before his fingers locked around my wrist and pulled me back to him. I landed on his lap, his hard cock pushed up against my back.

He said nothing as he shifted his cock under me, sliding into me quickly. I moaned as I felt his cock stretch my pussy walls. Killian gripped my hips, slowly moving me up and down. One hand wrapped around my throat, squeezing slightly as his other arm moved around my hips to hold me there. His fingers dug into the side of my throat, causing a spark to shoot down my body to my toes and up to my pussy. My pussy throbbed around his cock as he moved me up and down. He was in me so deep that I couldn't think of anything other than his mouth on my neck, his fingers on my neck and his cock deep in me. He grunted in my ear as he held back his own finish. I could feel his hand from my hips travel down to my clit, slowly rubbing as I groaned, tossing my head back on his shoulder. I tried to move my neck but his hand cut off my breathing every time. I laid my head back on his shoulder and let him move me the way he wanted me. I was completely at his mercy and I was honestly totally okay with that. I wanted to relish every goddamn move, the way he felt inside of me, the way my body moved in tune with him. I hated to think of the way his body seemed to be a perfect fit for my own.

Like we were meant to be.

Because this wasn't meant to be a kind of deal. In the morning, he'd be gone and I would be heartbroken again. I needed to put my shields up with no access to my heart.

Even though I knew that was impossible.

Killian squeezed my throat again and snapped me back to the present. His cock plundering its way for gold. A groan escaped from my throat as I started to rotate my hips on his lap. Killian groaned loudly in my ear as he fucked me from below.

Within moments, Killian had flipped me over onto my stomach on the bed and pulled my hips up. My ass was in the air. I tried to pull myself up but before I could, I felt his hand on my back, keeping my face down on the bed. His cock slammed into me from behind. Killian's hand wound into my hair and pulled back, lifting my head off the bed. The pull from the action caused my throat to push against my skin. Breathing was difficult but it didn't scare me. I knew he wouldn't hurt me, but I don't think he had ever fucked me this hard before. I hated to admit it, but I didn't hate it. I shoved my hands down on the bed and hefted myself up. It made it easier to breathe, and yet his cock was causing me to gasp in exhilaration.

He let go of my hair, the hand grasping my hip before it moved down and around to my clit. I screamed out as his finger rubbed my over sensitive little nub. Killian continued at my clit as he slammed into me. With both rhythms, my mind was going into overdrive as my pussy began to pulsate. I gripped the sheets as my pussy throbbed around his hard cock. Killian let out a strangled moan as I began to fuck his cock by moving my body up and down. I'd never needed anything so much in my life. But I needed his cock.

Finally, I tumbled over the edge, my pussy exploding around his cock as he continued to work my clit. I shoved his fingers away when it got too much as I landed down on the bed, face first. I was sucking in the sheet into my mouth with my deep breaths but I didn't care. Killian gave me a few seconds to recover before he flipped me onto my back and pulled my hips up, sliding his cock into me again, his face hovering over mine as he slid his body against mine. His lips claimed mine in a hard kiss, before he pummeled into me. A couple of thrusts and he was bursting into me, pump after pump. His face contorted into what could only be explained as a pained expression.

Slowly, he rolled onto his back, his cock still hard as he breathed hard next to me, his eyes closed. I wasn't sure I'd be able to walk just yet so I laid there next to him, looking at the pure beauty that was Killian O'Farrell.

The man I had always loved, no matter how hard I tried to ignore it.

And now, I knew I was well on my way to having my heart broken again.

———

THE COFFEE WAS WARMING me up just perfectly this morning. I'd left Killian asleep in the bed and crept out to the kitchen to fuel my brain. I had no idea why he had come to Dublin but it couldn't be good. I didn't want the O'Farrell wars to spill out into Dublin when I just moved here. If I'd wanted him gone, I could have easily called Sinead and she and Darren would have come over with reinforcements but I knew Killian would take off soon, with the last remnants of my already broken heart. I looked out the window of my dining room, onto the street below and wondered if it was worth waking him and telling him to leave. I knew he would if I asked him to, that was something I could always be assured of. He always listened to me.

Surely his presence hadn't gone unnoticed. Dublin was controlled by the O'Farrell's as with all Irish cities but they were rarely here, and no one from their businesses were out here to keep it in check. I had a feeling Dubliners didn't much care for the power they exerted.

My phone dinged. I checked it to see Sinead's name pop up.

SINEAD

Are you coming to work today or did I drink you under the table?

SLOANE

I'll be in later. I just need to take care of some stuff. I have an appointment. Sorry.

SINEAD

Okay. Let me know if I can help.

I sent her a thumbs up and put my phone back down. I hated to do this to her on the second day of work but I couldn't exactly tell her Killian O'Farrell was here. She even hated him back in the day when we had been dating. I could only imagine how much she hated him now and would desperately disapprove.

My chest tensed when I heard footsteps around the hallway. I looked over to see Killian walking out, his pants on but he was shirtless. The tattoo of his family crest on his chest stood out in the daylight. He had multiple other tattoos all around it but they'd come after I had known him. I still remember the day he'd shown me the tattoo his father had forced all his sons to get.

"Hey," I said. He smirked over at me, fully aware of what that smirk did to me. I got up from the chair at my table and moved over to the kitchen to keep my idle hands from reaching out for him. "Coffee?"

"Only if you make it properly."

I rolled my eyes before I pulled out a bottle of Irish Whiskey and made it exactly how he loved it. Killian relaxed into the chair. I hated how at ease he was in my apartment, and I especially hated how damn good he looked in the chair.

I finished his coffee and put it down in front of him before I sat back down, opposite him. "What are you doing in Dublin?"

His smirk dissipated and he took a sip of his coffee. "Why would you think it wasn't just because of you?"

I rolled my eyes but my heart secretly wanted to hear that it was for me. I was doomed.

"Be serious."

"I need you to come back with me."

I felt the laugh bubble to the surface before I could stop it. "Killian, you told me to leave and now you're telling me to come back?"

"I thought it would be safer here but it turns out, it's not."

"What are you on about?"

Killian put his coffee mug down and leant forward. "I found out someone you know is working for Ronan O'Brien. You're in danger."

"How am I the one in danger?"

"Because the man who Ronan trusts is Darren Lewis."

The sound of Sinead's husband's name had chills going down my spine.

"You think my own family are going to hurt me?"

"How well do you really know Sinead?" he asked me. I hated that the answer wasn't well, but I didn't want him to put doubt in my mind. Killian had been gone from my life for years, almost a decade, I didn't need this right now.

"Get out," I said.

"Slo."

"No, Killian, you can't just come in here, and tell me to come home after you told me to leave. Now, I have to leave because you're putting me in danger, yet again."

He closed his eyes, annoyed. Good.

"Sloane...I can't protect you if you don't listen to me."

"I'll be fine," I told him. "Darren would never hurt me and he'd never be involved with someone like Ronan. He's a good guy. I don't even think he's held a gun."

The sound of a knock on my door had Killian standing up and looking for what I could only imagine was a weapon. It was in the other room with the rest of his clothes but I wasn't going to make it easier for him to scare the hell out of whoever it was at my door.

"Relax."

I moved to the door, my heart raced as I looked up at Darren. "Are you all right?"

I nodded, even though I knew something was about to happen, but I couldn't put my finger on why I felt that way. Even though I had been ignoring Killian's pleas, I knew he wouldn't have come here unless some sort of fear was there. "Sure am."

He turned to come in and that's when he saw Killian.

"Hey," he aimed at him. "You're not welcome here."

"Darren, I presume."

I was about to move in between them before I felt Darren's hand on my arm. He held me in place beside him.

"Let her go," Killian growled.

"I don't think so," Darren replied, equally gravelly. I looked up at Darren, only to see his kind eyes change instantly. I felt incredibly vulnerable and like an idiot. I was entirely too far away from Killian for him to help me. How the hell had I gotten myself in trouble again?

He had been right.

No matter how far I got away from him, I was in danger.

What the ever loving fuck?

"Darren?"

"Sorry, Sloane, I really didn't want you to find out about it like this," he said, turning to me. He pulled a gun from the back of his belt and held it toward Killian.

I knew that wouldn't stop him. Killian didn't care if he got shot, he was fearless and that was why I had been so scared growing up. It was also why everyone was so scared of him, and not his brothers. I tried to move around so the gun was aimed at me but it was like Darren knew what I was doing. He yanked me around so I was in front of him, my back to his chest, as he held me in place with one arm around my neck, the gun at my temple.

Killian backed up, his hands up in surrender. Instantly, the calm assassin was backing away, unsure of what to do.

I'd never seen him so at a loss before and it was breaking me. He really did love me. How could I have been so fucking stupid?

Before I could speak again, something flew through the windows and landed on the ground. I screamed as the grenade looking things started to let out a thick smoke. Killian made a move to get to me before I felt Darren pulling me out of the apartment and down the stairs by the neck. I screamed out for Killian but Darren's arm around my neck cut it off before I could make much noise.

Darren shoved me toward a car, I kicked at his knees before I tried to run, only to collide with rock hard abs. I fell back, looking up into the eyes of Ronan O'Brien and his sick smile.

"Long time no see, Sloaney. I hate that it's come to this

but it's really your own fault for getting involved with him again."

I had no time to respond before I felt something slam over my mouth, and my eyes started to droop closed as I lost consciousness.

CHAPTER NINE

KILLIAN

"Killian?"

I cracked open my eyes, and coughed up the shit I'd inhaled when they gassed the apartment. Lorcan knelt beside me, trying to help me into a seated position.

"Did he take her?" I asked, my voice groggy.

"Yes," he said, gravely. "We weren't downstairs. Considering how long you were taking, we decided to get some food. Came back to this place smashed to pieces."

I looked around and saw they had ransacked the place, probably for a cover story. I was lucky they hadn't set it alight while I was passed the fuck out. My anger stewed at losing her again. The look of terror in her eyes as she realized I had been right and she had walked back into danger unwittingly had torn me in half. I got to my feet and proceeded to look around at the damage. The windows were all blown in, shards all over the once pristine carpets, tables had been overturned and the legs broken.

"Have you got any leads on this fucker?" I asked my older brother.

"You know we haven't. We only just got-"

I had my brother up against the wall, my forearm against his throat. "You were supposed to have my fucking back."

"We do," Lorcan said with ease. He'd always known how to overpower me, as children and still now as adults. "Always, but you should have had your piece on you. You knew the risks."

I took my forearm away and turned away, wondering how the fuck this could have gotten so bad. Ronan was fucking with the wrong family.

"Where do I go from here?"

"Think like the assassin, Killian," Lorcan said. "They call you the calm assassin for a reason. Don't think about the stakes, think about the fucker you want to take out."

He was right. I hated that he was always right but I couldn't let my feelings for Sloane cloud my judgment or she'd be killed.

She was the last semblance of humanity I had left, without her, I would be a fucking monster. A demon, no one would be able to come near. I'd become my father and that was one thing I couldn't bear to be.

"Where's Conor?"

"He's calling everyone he knows to find out where they've taken her."

"Get the cousin. Sinead. She's in on this, I know she is."

Lorcan nodded. "On it, you take five and get your shit together. The boys don't need to see you hanging on by a tether."

I nodded and waited for him to leave before I swung

around the empty apartment and planted my fist through the wall. When I pulled it out, half the wall came with it, including a long wire. Looking down at it, I saw it was leading through the thin wall and toward the TV.

I knew exactly what I was looking at. The fucker was recording her. I yanked the cord out of the wall, watching a unit on the top of the TV to fall back. I moved over to it and pulled it up, looking at the red light. It was muted, and probably hidden by a decoration on the TV so it didn't arouse suspicion but it was definitely a device you could see and hear in this place.

How long had they been planning this?

I got close to the device, making sure they could see me.

"You messed with the wrong brother, O'Brien. This shit is personal. I'm coming for you."

I threw the device to the ground and stomped on it before I grabbed my shit and headed for the door, angrier than I could have ever imagined I would be.

He'd woken a beast, and until I had my girl back, no one was safe.

SLOANE

I LISTENED in on the conversation outside the door. My wrists were bound, a big chain leading to the floor. All I could do was sit on the bed and wait. The chain had been resting on my leg and it had been freezing but I'd been able to shift my body just enough so that the heavy thing wasn't touching me. I heard Darren's voice and another who I could only assume was Ronan. It had been a while since I'd seen or heard from Ronan so it was tough to say.

My heart knew I should have believed Killian, after all, he came all the way to Dublin to warn me. If only those goddamn arms, eyes and body hadn't distracted him from his cause, we'd both be safe. I knew he would come for me, and honestly, I hoped he didn't. I wouldn't know what to do with myself if he got hurt trying to rescue me.

All I could do was try and find information and get a way to feed it back to him. My exhaustion was starting to hit hard though and I knew sleep was needed to get me through the next ordeal. They hadn't even checked on me since I woke up so I assumed I was a bargaining chip.

As if on cue, the door opened and I felt my mouth slide open in shock when I looked upon my cousin Sinead.

"I'm sorry it came to this," she said, her uplifted and sweet voice gone. Instead, she spoke with a harsh tone, just like one my mother had used on me when she hadn't been happy with me.

"You called me to Dublin to kidnap me?"

"No," she replied quickly. "I really didn't think you would come. You've always been so attached to that damn town. In fact, when you did decide to come, we had to move up our plans."

"What plans? Why do you even care about the O'Farrell's, they don't have anything to do with Dublin."

"And that took years to rid their power over this city. Soon, they'll be removed from Ireland and then the real fun begins."

"So you get rid of one family in power to replace them with another? You know what power does, right?" I asked, getting angry.

"The O'Farrell's had no right to take over in the first place."

"What are you talking about?"

"You really don't know the town's history, do you?" Sinead replied, a sly smirk appearing on her face. I knew that smirk. She'd always used that right before she was about to do something mischievous. "Poor little Sloaney, always seeing the good in people."

"The O'Farrell's aren't so bad, Sinead. You've never liked them and I have no idea why."

"Why should I?" she squared off with me, coming closer to the chains attached to the floor. "They ruined my daddy's business. They ran us out of town and we had to start over in Dublin, only daddy had to still pay them to do business here. I went to a shit school, and got next to nothing education to have a boring job that severely underpaid me and then there's you."

"Me?"

"You and your perfect face, skin and family. My own mother gave you her house, and I'm her only daughter. My entire life I've had to live up to the perfect Sloane Carpenter and now I'm the one that's wanted, the one that will have power and everyone will bow down to me."

That's when I realized just how bad this was. Ronan wasn't in charge. Sinead was and I had walked straight into her trap.

Fuck.

"Killian will come for me."

I don't know why I said it, I hadn't even realized I had been thinking it until it had been said.

Sinead smiled again. "I'm counting on it, Sloaney."

I hated it when she called me that and she knew it.

"When Killian comes in, looking for you, he'll get a bullet through the brain."

Fear flooded through me as the realization hit that I was

going to be the bait for them to take out the toughest O'Farrell.

Shit, fuck, shit.

Sinead headed for the door, turning back to face me in the open doorway. "Get comfy, cuz. You'll be here for a while."

She slammed the door shut and locked it. I slunk down on the bed, the chain clanking against each other as I felt the tears run down my cheeks.

I would be the reason Killian was killed.

Because I had fought against my feelings for him back when I was a kid, and now. I should have fought for him. I should have just told him I wasn't going to leave.

It was times like this I wish I was as headstrong as Teeghan.

KILLIAN

I TOSSED BACK the painkillers and thanked the nurse for her service. Lorcan took gassing and head injuries seriously, and somehow had forced me to come into the hospital to get checked out. My mind was still firmly on Sloane, and the only way I agreed was if someone was actively looking for them. Jeremiah had come down with one of Lorcan's men and was telling us about some property their father had bought a few years ago. He was going to take us there once I was done.

Hopefully it didn't take long before I had her in my arms, or so help me I would lose my shit. I felt like I was going to rage against Dublin, whether it was their fault or not.

Lorcan made his way over to me and thanked the nurse

who had walked me out. She was attracted to me, I could tell, and after years and years of sleeping with any woman who came my way, this was the first time I hadn't even been tempted to take her round back and have my way with her.

"Aidan has intel and he also has Jeremiah pointing him to a location," he said, putting his phone away. "We'll meet them there. Are you all clear?"

I nodded and he opened the door to the car. He got in behind the wheel and took over driving. I noticed Conor was nowhere to be seen.

"Where the fuck is Conor?"

"He's trying to convince his wayward woman to keep her nose out of the situation and go home."

"She followed us here?" I asked, surprised. Although, I didn't know why I was. Teeghan was as hard headed as all of us combined.

"You know she did. Not only is Conor in danger, but so is her best friend. I hate to admit it, but we need her kind of crazy."

I didn't want to admit it, but he was right. You didn't piss off Teeghan, she could emasculate the heartiest and most macho of men in seconds if she so pleased. In fact, I'd been impressed on more than one occasion but I'd never tell her that. I was the brother she liked the least, and I was okay with that.

Lorcan drove like a bat out of hell as we headed to the location. I fucking hoped Jeremiah wasn't lying. He wouldn't make it out alive if he weren't.

"How many men are coming?"

I grabbed my gun and made sure it was loaded, doing the same for Lorcan's piece.

"All of them," he said. "This needs to end. Ronan needs to get gone before we lose too many."

He was right. This shit had gone on far too long and without our knowledge. How could a new enemy be so strong already? This must have been years in the making.

My fingers tapped the side of my leg as we made our way through Dublin, and headed toward Meath. I was eager to see her again, but I was also eager to fuck Ronan up so good, no one would dare question our authority in Ireland again.

———

JEREMIAH AND AIDAN stood by their car outside a large country estate on the border to Meath and Dublin. Conor and Teeghan were there too, arguing in the car. That made me smile. Lorcan braced himself, making sure all of his guns were in their holsters and loaded before he joined us. Teeghan got out of the car, a gun in her hand, as she made her way over to us. Conor looked defeated. Now that was something I could understand.

"Tee."

"Don't even start with me, boy," she aimed at me. "You're the reason she put herself in harm's way."

"Me?" I squared off with her, causing Conor to come running over to us. "She's your friend. You couldn't convince her to stay?"

She wanted to hit me, I could see it in her eyes. Sloane had once told me that Teeghan wasn't someone you wanted to mess with, and I had seen glimpses of her anger but according to Sloane, I hadn't seen anything yet. I wanted that fiery woman to lash out so hard that all of Ireland would run scared when she came near. Tee wasn't scared of anyone, which was why Conor had gotten wrapped up in her from the beginning.

Conor put himself between us, and edged her away from me. She knew exactly how to rile me up and for once, I was thankful for it. I needed this anger to keep my woman safe.

"The place looks empty," Jeremiah said. "There should be cars here, Ronan doesn't travel alone."

He was right. That fucker always had a cavalcade of people around him. Safety in numbers I assumed.

"We need to check it out anyway," Lorcan said. Jeremiah simply nodded and pulled out his own gun. We took the house strategically, Lorcan and Conor with Teeghan behind to the side, Aidan, Jeremiah and me on the other side. Each of us looked in the windows and made sure we weren't going to be ambushed.

Lorcan signed to us that he would take the back with Conor and Teeghan. I led Jeremiah and Aidan to the front door, kicking it down with one of my hardest kicks to date. The door exploded with my kick, flying off the hinges and landing on the floor a few feet away. We entered, splitting up, our guns raised.

"Shoot anything that moves," I said to them. Moving down the hall, I unlocked the back door and let the others in before I checked the other rooms.

I got to the first room after I left the kitchen and kicked the door open. It swung open as if it had only been closed slightly and I stilled in my tracks.

My hand fell to my side as I moved inside, my eyes focused on the wall with three singular polaroid photos glued to the wall, surrounded by red scribbles all over the wall.

I smelt the copper before I could see it was blood. The fuckers had given me a message in blood. In the first photo, I saw Sloane chained to a bed, a dirty rag in her mouth to keep her quiet, her mascara running down her cheeks. The second photo, she had a bloody nose and cuts on her lips and eyebrows and in the third, she was naked, hovering in the corner of the room with her sick and twisted cousin laughing at her.

Lorcan grunted to let me know he was behind me as I turned to him, the message emblazoned in my mind:

"Nice try."

They knew we were coming. They knew Jeremiah would give the information up. They didn't know just what I was capable of yet. After seeing those damn photos, I knew the assassin was coming forth...only this time, he wasn't going to be calm.

I ripped the photos off the wall and pushed past Lorcan and out of the house so I could breathe. They were beating her and humiliating her...because of me. I never should have told her to go, I should have fought to keep her close.

I was a fucking idiot.

And she could die because of it.

I grabbed a lighter off Aidan who was standing by the porch and set the photos alight, tossing them to the ground and watching them burn until they were ash.

Teeghan came out of the house with Conor, her face ashen and her eyes staring off into the distance.

"What?"

"If he knew we were coming here, then he'll buckle down, right?" she said. "He'll go somewhere we will never find."

"We have to bring him to us," Jeremiah said from behind me. I turned around to see him coming to stand next to us. "A trade. He wants me dead, and he knows you won't do it. If you promise to give me to him for her, he will bring

133

her with the intent of never giving her to you, but she will be close enough you can get her."

"You'll be killed," Conor said.

"If that's what has to happen, then that's what happens," he said. "I'm sick of my brother and his twisted mind. He won't stop until he has ultimate power and that's not good for Ireland. You guys have always been what's good for Ireland, and he knows that."

I hated to admit it, but the guy was right. He will bring her to show her to me, but he'll use her against me. He wants me to lose control, he wants to show our townspeople that we aren't right for the job of looking out for them.

"Call him."

Conor wanted to turn and hit me but Jeremiah slunk off to call his brother. A call we didn't want to make but it was always going to be an option if it ever needed to be done.

"We can't let him walk into a death trap," Conor said to me.

"You think I want him to die?" I shot back at him. "But we are out of options and Sloane is running out of time. We don't have the upper hand, we don't even know how many hands we're going to need."

"We'll find a way to protect him," Teeghan offered but we all knew the chances of Jeremiah walking out of that meeting with his psycho brother was nil.

Jeremiah headed back up to meet us just as Lorcan came out of the house.

"He wants to meet at the docks, back home."

Conor immediately was on edge. That was his turf, not mine. This had to do with Conor somehow.

"Let's go home," I said, heading for the car. Lorcan was at my side almost instantly.

"You're thinking what I'm thinking?"

"Yes," I said. "But Conor can't know."

"Agreed."

We got in the car and thought of a plan of how to separate Conor from Teeghan. She was going to have to be the one to save Sloane and she would have to do it alone.

CHAPTER TEN

SLOANE

Sinead had been oh so kind to allow a doctor to come in and see me after she'd given me a beating the day before. I'd lost count the amount of times I'd been kicked and beaten since I'd been here, actually, I'd lost count how many days I had been here. They were all blending into each other. At least, they'd given me a dress to wear. I'd been naked for at least a day and it had been fucking cold. They hadn't broken me yet, though, and I knew it was getting to her.

"She's fine, a few broken ribs, but she'll live."

"Good," Sinead said. "Thanks, doc."

The doctor exited the room quickly, and I could tell he was a little scared of Sinead. I still couldn't believe the cousin I had grown up with was so wicked and held such ill regard for me. We'd been great friends growing up.

"Good news," she said, with the lilt of a child in her tone. "Your boyfriend has gotten in touch with Ronan and is looking for a trade."

Trade? What the hell was he going to trade?

"We're heading back to that little seaside town you love so much," she said. "You need to shower first, though."

I was already tense about this. Sinead wouldn't look this happy about losing her only bargaining chip. Immediately, I knew she had no intention of trading me for anyone. She was doing this to kill them. To get all the O'Farrell's together was a rare treat for any enemy. In one fell swoop, they could take out the O'Farrell dynasty.

Like hell I would let her.

She unlocked the chain around my wrists. Immediately, the weight of them fell off me and I felt freer than I had been for days. She pulled me up and allowed me to hobble to the bathroom I'd only seen the inside of a few times. For the most part, I'd had to use the bucket next to the bed.

Once inside, I looked at myself in the mirror and almost balked. I didn't recognise myself. So much so, I thought another person had been in the room. One of my eyes was half closed, a large cut was red and puckered over my eyebrow and two cuts were still bleeding over my lip. My face was dirty and bloody, my wrists red and sore. I had large welts on my arms and legs. I could only imagine what my body looked like under the dress.

"Ah, no you don't want to see that," Sinead said, and chuckled a little as she threw a hammer I hadn't realized she'd been holding into the mirror. It splintered, shards flying all over the room. I dodged a couple coming my way. Sinead pulled at the dress until it gave way and fell to my feet. She turned the taps on in the shower and tested the water. Her actions didn't make sense until I got under the spray and realized it was ice cold. I let out a shriek of shock as she laughed and closed the door to the shower, leaving me under the iciness of the water. The water pricked at my skin and I felt my entire body start to shiver as the blood washed away from me, going down the drain with efficiency.

"What the fuck are you doing?" I heard someone's voice say. "Get away from that shower stall."

Sinead groaned but she must have complied because the door opened quickly and I looked over at Ronan's angry face. He stuck his hand under the spray of water and realized just how cold it was as I fought the cold shivers my body was currently going through.

"I'm sorry," he said. He actually sounded like he was sorry as he turned the heat on and slowly, I started to warm up. "Get clean, warm yourself up and a fresh pair of clothes will be on the bed. I don't know what your cousin has against you, but it's a little sick."

"You think," I managed to spit out between jaw shudders.

"This was never about you," he said. "She told me that Killian would do anything for you, and so you became collateral damage. He'll come to the docks and we'll give you back to him for my brother."

"Your brother?" I questioned. "This was about him?"

"Well, yeah, he knows a lot of things I don't necessarily want the O'Farrell's to know."

"You tortured me for Jeremiah?" I asked him. "I'm not involved with the family. I don't know anything."

"I didn't torture you. In fact, I had no idea Sinead hated you so much until a few days ago. I'm sorry I didn't interrupt her deranged little fantasy but she serves a purpose. Finish up, we have a drive ahead of us."

The shaking had slowly eased and I felt warm enough to get out of the shower. A towel hung on the railing by the door. I could see my shattered reflection in the damaged mirror, the dark redness of my skin was unmistakable. I wasn't going to cry. I had cried enough. Now was time to get back home and find a way to protect Killian and his brothers.

The room was empty when I got back to the bed. The door was closed, but I knew Sinead would come back in soon enough. I got into the jeans and top which fit me like a glove and put the shoes that sat on the floor by the bed, on.

Slowly, I was building a tolerance for pain, and soon, I would make them wish they never set eyes on Killian O'Farrell.

KILLIAN

TEEGHAN WAS SITTING opposite me and Lorcan in the entertaining room. Her eyes focused on the floor. I didn't blame her. After coming up with the plan that Conor would have absolutely said no to, we knew she'd need to make the decision herself.

"You can say no," Lorcan said, sitting forward. "It's pretty fucking dangerous, but it's up to you."

"This will work, right?" she asked us. I knew she'd been through hell just a couple of months ago, being a hostage herself, and it made it harder to ask her to help us this time too, but I knew she'd not say no.

"We can't know that for sure," Lorcan offered. "But, even if it doesn't, you will be with Sloane."

She nodded, looking off to the empty fireplace. I could see the fear in her eyes and frankly, I didn't blame her.

"Conor will shit bricks."

"I know," I said. "But in the end, he will understand."

"No he won't," she turned back to us. "You better make sure he doesn't know the plan until it's been enacted."

"He can't know you're in the car with us," I said. "We need to put you in the boot."

"Perfect," she said, sitting back. "I'll do it. For Sloane."

I nodded, reaching forward and grabbing her hand. "Thank you. You know I wouldn't dare put you into this situation unless we had no option."

"Yeah," she said, putting her other hand on mine. "I know."

I released her and got up, moving out of the room, before I lost it. Conor was going to lose his shit when he found out the plan but hopefully it wouldn't come to that and we could easily extract Sloane without Teeghan having to get involved.

But knowing Ronan, things were only just going to get worse the second he rocked up. I sent out a message to the boys to be at the docks but to stay hidden. I didn't want them to think we brought an army with us.

I had so much anxiety bubbling inside of me that I could barely breathe. Soon, one way or another, Ronan would be back in town and we would have a shootout on our hands.

I just needed Sloane back.

SLOANE

Sinead was arguing with Darren in the front of the van. My hands were bound again, the rope rubbing against my wounds. At least the rope was far less heavy than the chains. If I held my hands up against my knees, I didn't feel any pain. My head was pounding though, and sleep was hard to come by when all I could hear was Sinead telling Darren what a loser he was. It was enough for me to wish sweet death on myself. How could anyone put up with that? Why would she stay with someone who she doesn't love? It's just a waste of life.

I could tell we were getting close with the way their arguing was intensifying. Not once had they checked on me, but that was okay. I would rather they spent more time arguing while I figured out a plan.

But what plan could I possibly construct while I was still injured and bound. I rested my head against the side of the van and waited for what I could only imagine would turn into a shootout.

It didn't take long before the van came to a stop. My heart rate began to speed up as I waited for the doors to open. Sinead and Darren both got out of the van, and I heard footsteps outside the back doors. I braced myself for whatever was coming.

The doors opened quickly and Sinead stood there, looking annoyed. She had a rag in her hand.

"Come on," she said, pulling my hands so I was forced to scoot forward, to the edge of the van. Before I could speak, she shoved the rag in my mouth and tied it behind my head, tight. My tongue was shoved down by the material in my mouth, and I was forced to breathe in and out via my nose.

"Don't try and speak, don't try anything," she said, angrily. "You'll get a bullet in the brain if you do."

I knew she would. I wouldn't make it far anyway considering my wounds.

I nodded slightly and she relaxed a little. She moved to the side where Darren was. They spoke in hushed undertones. I was able to look around me, even though it was dark and obviously nighttime, but I knew exactly where I was.

We were at the back of the docks. I saw the water, the

lights from the docks made the slight waves look ominous and yet inviting at the same time. Why the fuck would they bring me back to O'Farrell territory?

I was more concerned with their confidence. They wouldn't come here unless they thought they had an advantage.

When the cars started to roll in, I felt my fear rocket to the forefront. He was here...and they were walking into a trap.

KILLIAN

They were already at the docks when we pulled in. Conor didn't like it. He didn't like that the docks were being used as a trade. Jeremiah was nervous as fuck but I knew he would do what he needed to do.

Personally, I knew he was walking into his death, and he did too on some kind of level. My anger had risen all day once we'd gotten home and I'd done all I could at the gym to stay busy. I was itching to get my hands on Sloane again. This time, I'd never let her go.

But if things did escalate like I knew they would, we had a back up plan. One Conor couldn't know about. Lorcan pulled up next to us, and kept his lights on to make sure we had as much light as possible.

"Ronan isn't here."

I knew he was, but he just wasn't in sight.

"One of us should stay at the estate in case shit goes down," I said. "You know one of us needs to stay in charge."

Lorcan nodded. "Conor, go back to the estate and wait."

Conor wanted to fight it but he thought twice about complaining. He took Lorcan's car back to the estate. Once he was gone, I knew our plan could be enacted with no issues. Lorcan opened the boot of my car and let Teeghan out.

"Stay out of sight," I told her. "I mean it, Tee, they aren't going to allow any of us to get close."

She nodded and stayed behind us until something were to happen. Jeremiah was visibly shaking as he waited.

"They're keeping us waiting," I said to Lorcan.

"Relax," he replied. "They need to make the first move, they have what we want, remember."

It was hard to relax, and he knew I'd never be able to, but it was enough to annoy me that I focused my rage on the right people.

I was about to get up to pace when I saw a door open on one of the cars in front of us. Ronan, the cocky mother-fucker, got out and buttoned his suit jacket. He thought he was in control here. Sinead came to stand beside him, with Darren. The fucker who had taken Sloane from me in the apartment.

"Stop," Lorcan said, calmly.

I hated that he knew what I wanted to do.

"I can see a way to get over there," Teeghan said. "I'll stick to the shadows and go slow. You distract them."

"Be careful," Lorcan told her, softly, but loud enough for her to hear. She slowly moved back, toward the back of the car. I could see her slightly out of the corner of my eye but her doing her thing in the shadows had me even more anxious. We couldn't lose both of them.

"Are we doing this, gentlemen?" Ronan asked, throwing his hands out, confidently. He thought this was a game.

"Fuck this," I said. I pulled my gun and started to walk forward. Darren and some other fuckers came forward to protect their man.

"Too scared to face me yourself, O'Brien?" I yelled out. Ronan pushed in front of them, angry I had called him out. I was getting to the fucker.

Good.

"Bring him to me and we'll talk."

"Show me you have her and she's unharmed."

Ronan shrugged. "That isn't the deal."

Lorcan came forward. "He's not going to give her over to us. I doubt she's even here. He's being too cocky."

"Where are our guys?" I asked him, under my breath, without taking my eyes off Ronan.

"Kian called," Lorcan said. "They're held up. We only have a couple of guys around the place, hidden. Keep your attention on Ronan. I'll keep my eyes on everyone else."

"Where is my brother, O'Farrell?" Ronan called out. That's when I saw Jeremiah coming out from the shadows, his hands beside him and his shoulders relaxed. He knew what was coming before I could stop it.

I turned to Ronan who had his gun aimed and ready. The shot ripped out of the gun before I could react. Jeremiah fell to his knees, the bullet wound in the middle of his forehead. He was dead before his knees hit the ground.

CHAPTER ELEVEN

SLOANE

The shot came out of nowhere. First they were yelling, and then there was silence and then boom. My heart was in my throat. If it weren't for the gag, it may have leapt out of my mouth and run away.

I waited to be bundled back into the van but instead, there was an eerie silence for a few moments before gunfire erupted everywhere. I stood up and looked everywhere for somewhere to hide but I was in real danger of being shot no matter where I went. I got up the courage to try and make a run for it, shot or no shot, but that's when I saw her.

Sinead snuck up from beside the van and shoved me backward into the van again. I couldn't pull myself up before the doors closed.

Fuck.

I was so close.

The gunfire continued, followed by shouting and cars revving. Everything was happening so quickly, I tried desperately to get my wrists out of the ropes but they were so tight, I could feel my skin beginning to rip slightly.

I grunted in frustration as I felt the van rev to life. If I could get to the doors, I could probably force them open. In the rush, I know Sinead didn't lock them.

Pushing up to my knees, I was about to lean forward when the doors opened and I saw Teeghan. Relief flooded through me as she jumped inside and ran to me.

I was trying to show her we needed to jump out but she stopped me.

"We have to let them take us," she said quickly. "You need to trust me. Just let them take us, and I have a plan. If we jump out now, we'll surely be shot."

Sadness overwhelmed me as she slammed the doors shut again and the van drove off, forcing us to fall over ourselves. Teeghan ran to the side of the van and hid from the window where Sinead was screaming at Darren to go. She told me to stay where I was so they could see me.

I had no option but to listen.

"Run him over," Sinead screamed at Darren as the van sped through the parking area of the docks. That's when I saw Killian in the windscreen, aiming the gun at the window. I ducked, hoping he did shoot them but instead, I heard wheels screeching and then the gunfire was getting further and further away.

Tears freely flowed down my cheeks into the rag still tied around my mouth. I looked over at Teeghan who held her finger up to her mouth to keep me silent. Not that I could make sound even if I wanted to.

"What the fuck happened?" I heard Sinead scream.

"Ronan was always going to kill Jer. We need to figure out what his next plan is, Sinead."

"He did it so he couldn't tell them anything about our plan."

Sinead scoffed. "He told them already, I know he did. He was always a weak man. Thank fuck Ronan stopped telling him things early on."

"Whatever," Darren said, slamming his fist on the wheel. "Ronan keeps us out of the loop too, Sinead. Obviously, one day and probably soon, we'll be on the other end of his gun barrel too."

"Please," Sinead scoffed again. "He trusts us, well he trusts me."

Silence descended on the cab and I could see the cracks forming. Sinead thought she was in Ronan's inner circle, but he was a two faced snake and would turn on anyone he thought he had to in order to win. And he wanted to win over everything.

KILLIAN

I shot the last of Ronan's guys in the head and tossed his body over the edge of the dock, into the water. Turning around, I looked over at the body of Jeremiah and saw Lorcan issuing a prayer for him. I hadn't seen him do anything religious since we found out about the dastardly priest a few months ago.

"We should get back to the estate," I told him. "You were right, they were never going to give her back. Do you think she was even in that van?"

"Look around," Lorcan said, standing once more after he had closed Jeremiah's eyes. "Do you see Teeghan anywhere?"

I looked around the darkened dock and noticed she was

nowhere to be seen. Conor was going to lose his shit when we got back. Hell, he'd already be losing his shit.

"Grab Jeremiah's body and take him to the morgue. He did us a favor and he paid with his life for it. Now we have to trust Teeghan will pull off what she's planned."

I turned back to my brother. "We were in that room together, she didn't have a plan. She only just accepted the risk."

"After you left, she told me what she was planning."

Of course she did. They had a weird close brother and sister bond. It had made Lorcan almost bearable to be around these last few months but it annoyed the hell out of me and Conor that he trusted her more than us.

"What's her plan?" I asked.

"Just leave it. Conor is going to be an issue when we get back, and you know that. Let's deal with that first."

I wanted to punch him, to knock some sense into him, but that would only cause more shit to go down and right now I needed to find a way to get to Sloane.

"We could race after them," I offered. "We could catch up to them and take them."

"Both Sloane and Teeghan would be killed and you know that," Lorcan said. "Get Jer to the morgue."

I hauled Jeremiah up as Lorcan spoke to the boys who had been hidden around the docks. I couldn't help but feel a little annoyed that none of them could help with Teeghan and Sloane. I hefted Jeremiah up and pulled him toward the car. Lorcan had taken off with the other guys, leaving me alone at the scene of the crime. Conor was going to lose his shit, not just about Teeghan but about the fact his docks were covered in blood.

Once Jeremiah was in the back, I called Marty.

"Yeah?"

"Is that how you answer your fucking phone?" I yelled into the speaker.

"Oh shit, Killian, I'm sorry...what can I-"

"Get a gurney outside, I'm heading there now. I have a body for you."

"Ah yeah, sur-"

I cut him off and threw my phone on the floor of the car in anger. I was so fucking close. I should have fucking shot Ronan when I had the chance.

I should have done a lot of fucking things to stop this from happening. If our dad was still alive, there was no way in hell anything like this would have gotten this far.

We had to stop being so soft and start being a lot more like ol' Finneas.

I pulled into the parking area of the hospital and around to the back where the morgue doors were. Marty was waiting for us with a gurney, looking like the squirrelly fuckwit he always had been.

He headed over to the car and opened the side door as I got out of the driver's seat.

"Jeremiah?" he looked over at me, confused. "You want a proper burial for Jeremiah O'Brien?"

"He did us a favor," I said, lighting a cigarette. "Do it properly. Full respect, you understand?"

Marty nodded. "Who should I call?"

"Well, his brother was the one who shot him so I really don't know. Call Lorcan when he's ready to be picked up. He'll deal with it."

Marty nodded and pulled Jeremiah up on the gurney, closing the back door and taking him inside. I flicked my cigarette and got in my car, tearing through the streets until I got back to the estate.

Taking a deep breath after I cut the engine, I tried to

will myself into a calm state. I was going to need it while Conor lost his shit at me. I opened my glovebox and pulled out the little baggie I kept in here for nights with the women who wanted to let loose. I hadn't needed it much lately so I still had plenty in here.

I poured a little bit out, onto the side of my fist and sniffed up the white powder quickly. Sniffing back to make sure it went down, I sealed the baggie again and tossed it back in the box before I got out. Tasting the chemically taste at the back of my throat as the coke went down, I pushed the taste away as I headed inside.

The yelling was loud as Conor took it out on Lorcan. Lorcan remained quiet as I entered the room to see him sitting at the end of the table, letting Conor hammer it into him. Conor turned to see me standing there and he stopped yelling.

"What's the plan, dickhead?" he aimed toward me. "We need to fucking get them back. Why are we just sitting around?"

"You're right," I said. Conor was surprised enough he didn't know what to say.

"What?" Lorcan finally spoke.

"We need to stop being the three brothers who want to rule peacefully," I todl them. "Father never had these issues and you know why? People feared him, that's why. We need to do what needs to be done so our women are safe, and no one thinks they can overrun us."

"Killian..."

"Enough, Lorcan. You don't have a woman to protect. You don't get a fucking say in this."

It was a low blow, even for me, but it had to be said. I could see the darkening in Conor's eyes too. He knew exactly what I was talking about. He had probably been thinking the same thing.

"You can't change the way we do things," Lorcan said, standing up. "We worked our asses off to show them we wouldn't be like that. They were scared of our dad, and his men. A town in fear will never be the way to go."

"Then why is it that dad never faced this kind of shit? You've not been tortured and beaten to hell by them. Dad would never have that happen, Lor. We're too soft and now our women are in the middle of it."

"What would dad have done if mum had been taken?" Conor asked in a calm tone. A scarily calm tone that I knew was spring loaded for an attack.

Lorcan's tension relaxed because he knew it would have never happened. No one would have dared, but if they had, our father would have launched an attack so vicious, no one would dare to try anything again.

"It's time to harden up," I said. "You know we're right."

Lorcan sat back down, tense once more. He was relenting to us, and I knew it was because he knew the only way forward was to be seen as the power. The power who can look after our people.

The coke was active in my system. I could feel it already and I wanted to punch the fuck out of anyone who got in my way, brother included.

"You have to stay here," Conor said to Lorcan. "One O'Farrell at the helm, at all times. You know you have to stay."

Lorcan nodded. "Fine, but I want constant updates and don't be fucking going in half cocked. Take everyone, strategise."

I nodded and Conor joined me as we headed out to the car.

SLOANE

Teeghan had been texting on her phone for the last thirty minutes, as we traveled in silence. She kept her eye on where we were through the half boarded window in the back of the van. I couldn't believe she didn't just pull me out of the van at the docks.

She put the phone into her jacket pocket and zipped it up, before she checked through the window to the cab. It had been quiet for a few minutes as Darren drove us back to wherever the hell we had been. Teeghan slowly and quietly crept over to me and started to pull the knots out of the ropes around my wrists and pulled the rope free. She held her finger to her mouth to keep me quiet as she pulled the rag from my head.

"I need you to be super quiet and don't react," she whispered to me. "I have a plan. In about three minutes, we're going to jump and roll. You understand?"

I nodded, unsure of what the hell she could have planned.

"We can argue after we escape," she whispered. "For now, I need you to relax and listen to me."

I tried to breathe but my heart was hammering so much that I was starting to feel jittery. Teeghan took my hand in her own and tried to calm me down as she continually checked the window for Sinead to catch us.

"We got this," she whispered. "We just need to roll before we jump out. Don't jump with your feet, you need to sort of roll your body into the air and let yourself roll onto the dirt road. The hedges will hide us if they find out what we've done but we're about to head onto one of the worst roads in Ireland. The potholes will cover our escape."

I nodded, trying desperately not to think of what jumping out of a moving vehicle could do to my already battered body.

Teeghan glanced up at the window again, to ensure they hadn't seen her, and then she helped me to my feet.

"Wait," she whispered, as we hovered near the door, our bodies bent over, but I was already thinking of how I was going to spin my body into the air. "On three."

I nodded to her.

"One, two...three."

We kicked at the doors together just as the van hit a large pothole. I flew through the air, rolling to the best of my ability before I hit the ground hard, still rolling. Each roll on the ground hit some part of my body hard. When I finally stopped rolling, I felt like I couldn't move. The air was coming out of my lungs very weakly as my body ached from hitting the ground hard. The van stopped. I heard the massive brake and skid as they realized we had gotten out.

Sinead was going to come and kill me now. She had no use for me anymore. I closed my eyes, waiting for surely what was coming but instead, I felt myself being yanked to the side of the road. I landed in the ditch to the side of the road, the hedges scratching my skin. Teeghan put her hand over my mouth and told me to keep quiet as we hid amongst the bushes on the side of the road.

The pain in my body was hard to fathom. I didn't know how I hadn't passed out from the pain but here I was with a splitting headache, a body that didn't want to move and a best friend who was doing everything possible to get me out of this predicament.

I heard the tyres from the van screech down the road,

past us and Sinead yelling at Darren to do something. He was trying to placate her and tell her that they didn't need me anymore but she was hellbent on getting me back to Killian.

And that was exactly where I wanted to be.

Sinead and Darren finally got in the van and took off again.

"Can you move?" Tee asked me as she tried to look me over.

"I don't think so."

"No worries," she said, sitting down next to me in the bush. "Lorcan knows where we are. He has pinged my phone, so now, we just need to sit back and wait for help."

"Lorcan? Not Conor?"

"Conor didn't exactly sign off on me jumping in the van."

I chuckled, knowing just how much of a screamathon was coming when she got home. Poor Conor. All he wanted to do was keep her safe and she kept putting herself in danger.

"Is anything broken?" she asked me.

"I don't know, but I fucking hurt, that's for sure."

"You didn't look great before we jumped out of a moving van. I can only imagine what you're going to look like in the cold harsh light of the day."

"Thanks, Tee."

She giggled which made me chuckle even though that hurt me to do as well. When our laughing died down, I could feel tension reach between us.

"Is that a car?"

She looked up onto the road but ducked down quickly again. "It's not them. We stay down until we get a message."

I nodded, thankful I wouldn't have to move yet.

"So, what are you going to do when we get back?" she asked me. I could tell it was a question she'd been wondering herself.

"Heal."

She chuckled, but I could tell she wanted a real answer.

"I don't know, Tee. Honestly, at this point, I'm safer with Killian, and I know that but I know his reputation."

"He's not the guy you met in school?"

"He's darker than that guy," I told her.

"Aren't you darker than the girl you were back then?" Teeghan asked me. "You're not all sunshine and roses anymore."

That was true. I'd been through some real shit in the years after I had left Killian.

"Well, what do you want?" Teeghan asked. "Do you want a life away from the town you loved and grew up in or do you want to fight for the man who would do literally anything for you?"

A life without Killian...now that was no life at all.

I couldn't walk away...not this time.

"After everything," I said, finally. "Killian...fuck...Killian is my everything and I think he always has been."

"I thought so," Teeghan said with a smile in her voice. "Now, you and I both know how dumb he is, just like his brother. You may have to fight for him to understand that."

"I'm not letting him decide to send me away again," I told her. "And if he tries to reason with me, I'll remind him of what happens when I'm not near him."

Teeghan chuckled. "Thatta girl."

———

TEEGHAN'S PHONE vibrated and she picked it up and looked down at the message she'd just received.

"Okay, Lorcan is close by."

She grabbed my hands, and pulled me to my feet. My knees buckled a few times before I finally found the strength to be able to walk up onto the road again. Before I had to try, Lorcan appeared before us and he took over from Teeghan. Lorcan was strong, just like his brothers, and he lifted me into his arms with ease. He was looking at the injuries on my face with concern. It was so hard to believe this was the brother Killian once feared. He'd only ever been a sweetheart to me.

"Are you well? Do you need to go to the hospital?" he asked me.

"I don't know, all I know is I want to feel safe and right now I don't."

Lorcan nodded quickly and opened up the back door of his car and helped me in. I laid down on the seat, curling my legs up to fit on the seat. Lorcan closed the door and I heard he and Teeghan speaking in hushed tones outside but I couldn't be bothered to care right now.

Sleep was coming for me and for the first time in weeks, I wasn't trying to fight it off.

CHAPTER TWELVE

KILLIAN

"Lorcan just sent me a message to come home," Conor said as he pulled the car over on the side of the road. We'd been so close to catching up to Sinead and Darren, but Ronan had gotten away scot free yet again. That fucker was going to have to pay for the shit he'd done to us.

"Why?"

"Doesn't say," Conor said. "It's up to you. I'm with you."

It could be a false request. He might have news, but wouldn't he just text that? Fuck. I couldn't give up now. We were hot on the trail.

"Leave the phone," I told him. I pulled my own phone out and turned it off, throwing it in the back of the car. Conor shrugged his shoulders and followed suit before he started the car again and took off toward Dublin. We were almost there. I put my head against the back of my seat and tried to forget all the shit in my life that I regretted and focused on getting Sloane back.

Closing my eyes, I couldn't help but think back to the

time I was close to fighting for her back before she got married.

Sean was mowing the lawn of the house he was renting when I pulled up outside. I knew he'd been seeing Sloane, and truth be told, I didn't know enough about him to be anywhere near okay with it. Seeing Sloane laugh with another guy was painful. When I got out of my car, I lit my cigarette and leaned against the hood of my car. He turned the mower off and wiped the sweat from his brow with the back of his forearm before he made his way over to me.

I liked that he wasn't scared of me.

I knew he was Kennedy's son, and I never had a thing against the Kennedy's, but that may change in about five minutes' time.

"Killian."

"Sean," I replied.

"Any reason you've come by?"

He knew about me and Sloane, I could tell by the way he was looking at me defensively.

"I heard about you and Sloane."

"And?"

"She deserves the world, you know."

Sean nodded. "Yeah and I can give her more of a life than you ever could."

He was right.

"You have to know if you hurt her, I will come for you."

"She doesn't need you to protect her," Sean said. "She's got me for that now."

It was a challenge. I knew it, but I wasn't going to cut him down in his prime. I did need someone to watch over her and if she wanted to be away from my family business, then I had to walk away.

"You don't want to make an enemy of me, Sean."

"Are you threatening me?" Sean asked, a smirk on his face. He was looking for a fight. He wanted Sloane to hate me and a slug to her new man's face would certainly do it.

"Yeah, I am. If I see that woman in tears, I'll be coming for you."

I dropped the butt of my cigarette on the ground and got into my car as he made his way back over to the yard. I revved my car and sped off, to get his challenge out of my mind. I have never wanted to beat someone's ass so bad in my life and I was fighting every urge in my body to turn around and go to do that but I didn't want to hurt Sloane.

I never wanted to hurt that woman again.

She had my heart, and I knew it.

There would never be another woman to replace her.

I pulled into the row of shops near the bay, mostly so I didn't turn around, but I knew I'd come here for a reason, even if I hadn't actively been thinking about it.

Getting out of the car, I walked into the tattoo shop and looked around. Two burly looking men, fully tatted, looked up at me. From the look on their faces, they knew who I was.

"Can I help you?"

The question came from a woman. I looked over to see a heavily tattooed woman making her way behind the counter.

"Sure, do you work here?"

"Yeah, I own this place."

"I need a tatt."

"Sure, did you know what you want?" she asked. I could tell by the way she was leaning over to show me her full cleavage and the lilt in her voice that she wanted me. I should be flattered, she was attractive, but I was hellbent on getting my head around the fact that Sloane had moved on and I needed to do it too.

"It's a name."

"Your girlfriend?" she asked, looking even more sultry.

"My ex."

"We don't tend to do those," she said. "Because we don't want you to come back and be pissed about it later."

"I'll sign whatever you want. I just need it done."

She nodded. "Sure. No need to sign anything. Come on over, the last chair."

I moved past the half closed curtain and past the two guys getting their legs tatted. The woman came over and got her machine ready. I pulled my shirt off and looked for a spot to put the name.

"Wow," she gasped as she turned back to me. "That tattoo is intense."

I looked down at the tattoo I had on my chest. The same one my brothers had, and the same my father had. Our family crest sat in the middle of my chest, with celtic knots all over our pecs that led up to our shoulders. There was a spot or two under my pec where I could get the tattoo done. Not many would question it when they saw it, because it wouldn't be the center piece but I would know it was there and that was all that mattered.

"Here," I pointed to the area free from ink. She nodded.

"You're Killian, aren't you?" she asked as she pushed the button on the end of her pen.

"Yeah."

"I'm Tash. Just call out if you need me to slow down but judging by this ink, I doubt you'll have an issue."

"Just do it. Her name is Sloane."

I spelled it out for her and she nodded. "I'll do it justice."

She probably thought she was dead and I was putting her name on me because I wanted to remember her, but I knew this was the only way I would be able to keep her.

The needle began to hit my skin and I closed my eyes, relishing the feel of the pain hitting my chest. I didn't want to admit to anyone but I loved getting tatts. The pain was a huge turn on.

The way Tash was biting her bottom lip, I knew I was going to be able to get rid of the boner I was about to pitch from the pain.

What better way to say adios to Sloane than by fucking another pussy?

CONOR NUDGED me and woke me up from my memory slash dream. "We're here."

I looked around at the sunrise setting over the hill and the apartment block that I knew Sinead lived in. We'd done our recon when Sloane was going to move down here and I'd looked up shit on her cousin but she had hidden her associates well. I'd not seen one fucking thing to warn me about what Sloane was walking into.

"Let's go inside."

I followed Conor inside, keeping my gun beside me, on full alert. The apartment was dark, and I already knew they weren't here.

"Where the fuck would they go?"

"They dropped the van off," Conor said. "It was down-stairs. So they did come back at some point but Sloane definitely isn't here."

"They wouldn't keep her here," I said. "Lorcan's guys already checked this place out before."

Conor picked up a folder and flicked through it, pulling a piece of paper out and looking at it.

"What is it?" I asked him.

"It looks like a list of members that work for Ronan."

"Really?" I replied, going over to look at it. For months we had been trying to get information on his operation and there'd been literally nothing to find.

"I'd say it was done by Sinead. Maybe she was trying to overtake them and had to create her own track record."

"Sinead has always been someone who wanted the best of everything. Even when she was younger, nothing her parents ever gave her was enough. She was always stealing other people's limelight."

"So sabotage?"

"I wouldn't put it past her."

I noticed a name on the sheet that had my blood running cold. Snatching the piece of paper out of Conor's hands, I looked down at the name.

"Amity."

Conor's eyes widened. "Shit. How the hell could she possibly be involved?"

"I don't know, but this shit needs to be figured out and fast. I can't leave Sloane with them any longer."

"Teeghan is with her, you think I'm not doing everything I possibly can?"

He was right. I put my hand on his shoulder and gave him the piece of paper back. "Get everything you can see. We need to figure out where to go next."

Conor nodded and grabbed the rest of the pieces of papers on the table and we headed back to the car.

"What?" Conor asked as I waited, impatiently, for him to get in the fucking car.

"Just hurry up."

Conor finally slid in and I took off down the street and parked far enough away to watch. Conor was about to ask me why we'd stopped again when the explosion went off.

The apartment exploded into fire, glass shattering all through the streets.

"What he fuck?"

"They need to know that we're coming."

Conor nodded. "Sure, but there could have been more information in there."

"I doubt it."

Conor went back to looking through the papers. "There's another address here, but it's in Meath."

I started the car and headed toward Meath.

SLOANE

Teeghan was sitting in the chair next to my bed with a magazine in her hands. The beeping told me I was probably in need of some kind of surgery but as I looked around, I knew I was at the estate.

"Hey," I said, but almost didn't recognise my voice. It was gravelly, as if I hadn't spoken in days. Teeghan put the magazine down and smiled as she sat forward and pressed a button on the side of the bed.

"Where am I?"

"The estate," she said. "Did you know they have a hospital room here? Walter is a doctor. I had no clue until they brought you here. When Lorcan tried to take you to the actual hospital, you had a massive tantrum."

I tried to pull myself up but she held me back. "No, you need to relax. You had a lot of bruises on your body. I don't even know how the hell you didn't have anything broken. Walter thinks you'll take a few weeks to get better."

"How long have I been here?"

163

"Four days," she said. "You were asleep for a long time. I was getting worried."

"Killian?"

Teeghan sighed and sat back in her chair. "No, both he and Conor are still looking for Sinead and Darren and Ronan. Their phones are off too but Lorcan explained that they had a bit of a falling out when I stowed myself away in the van with you."

"Conor was probably going nuts."

Teeghan sighed and rolled her eyes. "Ok, mum. Well, I'm glad you're awake. Get some rest, I'll come by a little later."

I nodded and closed my eyes as she left the room again. Hopefully the next time I woke up, Killian would be here and I could tell him everything I'd been going over for the past few weeks. I needed him to know that I chose him.

———

IT HAD BEEN over a week since I had returned to town, and to the estate, but Killian hadn't come back. I hoped like hell that he knew I was here and he wasn't going on a suicide mission, taking his little brother with him. I moved down the stairs and toward the kitchen. I'd been eating but not nearly enough to sustain myself. Sleep had been a welcome stranger since I got back and it had been all I'd wanted to do.

"Sloane?"

I spun around to see Lorcan coming out of the office, a worried expression on his face.

"Hey Lorcan," I replied. "I was just looking for some food."

"Ah," he said, coming over to me. "You're feeling better?"

"Much," I replied, as he led me into the kitchen. "I didn't sleep much when I was...well, you know."

"That's understandable."

He opened the fridge and pulled some things out, while turning on the stove.

"Lorcan, I can cook for myself."

"Nonsense," he said. "You're a guest."

He did something next that I hadn't seen, well not at least for several years. He smiled. The weary lines from around his eyes crinkled and his eyes lit up. He seemed so much younger when he smiled but having Killian and Conor as brothers couldn't have been easy on him.

"Have you heard from them?"

The smile was gone and the same old Lorcan was back.

"No," he replied. "But you know Killian, he's better at this than any of us. He'll be fine."

"You're still worried, though?"

Lorcan sighed. "Of course, they are my brothers. I'm more concerned with the fact Killian doesn't know you are safe."

My stomach dropped. "You didn't tell him?"

"I tried to," he said as he dropped bacon into the pan. The sizzle snapped my attention to what was happening in the kitchen. "He turned his phone off."

"Is there another way to get the news to him? Someone who can track him down?"

"There are a number of our men doing that as we speak," Lorcan said. "The only problem is when Killian wants to do something that we don't all agree on, he knows how to avoid being tracked."

Lorcan went to work on the eggs next and popped bread

into the toaster. I couldn't seem to think about anything other than Killian, even though the smell of the breakfast was divine.

"Sloane," Lorcan broke my spell and I looked over at him. "You need to let me worry about him and Conor. Your main job here is to relax and recover, yeah?"

I nodded and offered him a smile but it wasn't genuine and I knew he could tell. He went back to cooking, and then plated it all up.

When it was in front of me, I couldn't help but be impressed.

"This looks like a chef prepared it," I said, picking up my fork. "Who knew you were so handy in the kitchen?"

"We all have hobbies," he said, as he started to clean up. "Eat up."

"Where's Teeghan?"

"She's gone to the docks," he said.

"Why?"

Lorcan stilled before he dropped all the dirty pans in the sink. Slowly, he turned around and rested against the bench.

"You know, being with Conor, she is prone to dangers that we face, but also information about how we run things."

I shrugged. "Well, yeah, I figured."

"Conor is away, which means we are down men. Teeghan has been learning how to run the business while he is away."

That was news to me.

"Oh."

"Can I ask you a question?" he asked after a brief pause.

I nodded as I plowed into my eggs.

"You broke up with Killian because you never wanted this life," he said. "You're here...involved with him again.

You do know his life hasn't changed, in fact, he's more in than he was back then."

It was valid, something Teeghan had been asking me about too. Over the last couple of weeks, I had thought about it and why I couldn't seem to walk away from him again.

"You know, Lorcan, when I broke up with Killian, I was eighteen. I still loved him but I was, well let's just say I was a little green. I was sunshine and roses as Teeghan calls it. I didn't like death or crime, but look at what I've gone through since then."

Lorcan nodded. "You'd be okay with Killian doing what he does?"

"Yes," I said, confidently. "Because, Lorcan, there are a lot of bad people out there. I had no idea how evil and cruel people could be until recently. I'm not a doe eyed eighteen year old anymore, and truth be told, I never expected to marry someone else. I broke up with him because-"

"You thought he would walk away from the business."

I nodded. "I did."

"You have to know it wasn't that he didn't want you," Lorcan said. "Our father had a pull over us that none of us could deny."

"I remember," I told him. "He was fucking scary. Killian would never allow me to be anywhere near him."

"He was an asshole and he treated women like his own personal maids, except for our mother. All of us decided never to bring women home to meet him after..."

"After what?"

Lorcan sighed. "He took advantage of a situation when we were younger."

"Okay, Lorcan, I need a little more than that."

"It doesn't matter," he said, pushing up off the kitchen bench. "It's in the past."

I pushed my plate to the other side and he put it in the sink.

"What's there to do in this big ass place?" I asked, looking around. Lorcan chuckled before he rinsed the plate and put it on the side of the sink to dry.

"Well, we have a couple of big TV's, all the streaming services you could want, or you can go down to the bay. We have a boathouse you can chill in or you can go into the library, my mother kept a million books."

"I didn't know you guys had a houseboat."

"They don't. I do. I can take you out if you like, get some peace and quiet."

"I think we both know that you have to stay here."

His smile disappeared. "You're right. Well, you have run of the house, Sloane. Holler if you need anything."

He started to move away, out of the kitchen, when I grabbed his arm. He turned to face me, his face full of concern.

"He slept with your girlfriend, didn't he?"

He smiled but I could tell it was forced. "You're very perceptive."

"I'm sorry that happened to you."

"Like I said...it was a wake up call for us," Lorcan said, putting his wall up again. "And it's not like its an issue anymore."

"Killian protected me from him, just like you would have protected her from him if you knew," I told him. "Lorcan, you have the weight of the world on your shoulders, the eldest brother, the one who was meant to take over, but you don't have to do this alone. It's time for you to find someone to share the burden with."

"Welcome to the family, Sloane."

He kissed me on the forehead and went back into his office. I felt the pain in his voice and I desperately wanted to help him but this was something he had been holding on to for years, over a decade.

It just made me realize how much Killian did for me. He risked us, our happiness, all those years ago, to protect me. By the time Finneas had died, I was with Sean.

God.

Why didn't he just tell me what was going on with him?

Tears threatened. In the past I had been clueless about, which had led to all of this. It was a funny way to discover we were meant to be…but I'll take it.

KILLIAN

The house was only a stone's throw from where we had found the photos of Sloane before. The lights were on in the living area, I could see Sinead walking around, and Darren sitting down in front of the TV. Sinead seemed to be on the phone, throwing her hands around erratically.

"What are we going to do with this list?" Conor asked me as I lit another cigarette. "You need to quit that shit."

"Fuck off, it's helping me."

"No, it's not. I thought you quit anyway."

"Yeah well recent events have made me want to take it up again, so sue me."

Conor shook his head as he flipped through the pages again.

"Cathal is down the street, watching us, why don't you take it down to them and get them to take it Lorcan."

Conor turned in his seat and looked down the street at

the black car Lorcan's men had been waiting for our next move in.

"How long have they been with us?" Conor asked.

"A few hours. I guess they've been looking for days so that's a credit to us that we kept them guessing that long."

"Ronan may have people in that house we haven't seen," Conor said. "We should get Cathal to help us."

"The way she is flailing about, she's trying to explain something. They're on the out with Ronan."

Conor put all the papers back into the folder and got out of the car. I watched as he kept to the shadows and headed down to Cathal. It wasn't long before Cathal was driving off and Conor came back without the folder. I got out of the car, and prepped my gun. We both headed toward the house, and quickly moved around to the back. Conor worked the lock on the back door and we entered the house as quickly as possible.

Conor took the rooms to check if we were alone with them. Sinead was screaming into the phone while Darren flicked through the TV channels, bored. Conor headed in through the kitchen, bending down to take the shot. I nodded and he shot into Darren's skull. He dropped the remote he'd had in his hand. Sinead finally shut up and turned around to see her husband laying lifeless in the recliner. She dropped the phone and tried to look for a weapon or even to find where we were but both Conor and I knew how to keep ourselves hidden in plain sight.

Sinead walked straight into the kitchen where we both were. I raised my gun and pointed it at her head. She stopped in her tracks, her eyes wide in fear.

"Ple-" she started but my finger squeezed the trigger before she could finish. The bullet entered right between her eyes. She fell to the floor, dead instantly.

I walked over to the phone she had dropped, hearing the screaming voice on the other end. Picking it up, I held it to my ear, a smile appearing on my face when I heard who was screaming.

Ronan.

"Sinead can't come to the phone right now."

Silence.

"I'm coming for you."

Ronan hung up without another word and I threw the phone to the floor. I grabbed Sinead's body and dragged her by her arm into the living area.

"What are you doing?" Conor asked, putting his gun away.

"Go and see if they left anything here," I told him. Conor knew better than to argue with me. He moved away, as I bent down and dipped my fingers into her bullet wound. The blood pooling there was enough for me to do what I needed to do.

I started to swipe my bloodied fingers down the wall until I had spelled out the message I wanted Ronan to find.

"Tick, Tock"

CHAPTER THIRTEEN

KILLIAN

Sloane was asleep in my childhood bed. I didn't want to wake her up, judging from the injuries on her face, she needed to rest. I hated to see her like this.

It only made me angrier that they had dared to hurt her to get to me. Conor motioned for me down the hall to come with him. I closed the door quietly and headed down the stairs to the dining room. Lorcan was sitting at the head of the table.

"I tried telling you," he offered before I could speak. I knew he would have, but he should have tried harder. Although, I didn't regret what I'd done. Ronan needed to know I wasn't the one he could mess with.

"What's in front of you?" I asked, preferring not to get into a fight with him. I hadn't slept for days, and I was tired. I didn't want to talk about Sloane, not with what I was fighting with in my brain right now.

"These are the files you stole from Dublin. Cathal delivered them not long before you returned."

"And?"

"It appears to be a list of properties, contacts and a list of members loyal to Ronan. This does appear to the honeypot."

"Good."

Lorcan leaned back in his chair, just like our father did, and yet he couldn't be further from Finneas. He was the soft side of him, the one no one but our mum saw. I was the aggressive side of him that his enemy's saw, and Conor was the reckless side that he showed when a family member was in danger.

All of us made up our father.

But our father would never had let it get this bad. Our own town was starting to see the cracks in our power over them and once that goes, we lose the empire our great grandfather started. Once we lose power, we're all in greater danger than we already are now.

"We can't just go in, guns blazing, leaving blood messages on walls with executed members laying underneath it."

He knew?

Already?

"Ronan sends his regards and a few threats," Lorcan replied. "You really need to pull your head in, Killian. Dipping your finger into an open wound to write a message...it's sick, you know that, right?"

"Is that all?" I asked.

"Guys," Conor said, breaking the tension. "Can we focus on Ronan for a few more minutes? He's fucking attacked Teeghan, and Sloane. No matter what we do, they will always be in danger until he's taken out."

"It's not just him," Lorcan said. "He has an operation

behind him, one that will continue without him at the helm. We have to take them down, one by one."

"How do we take down an entire operation if we don't know who to attack?" Conor asked the obvious question.

Lorcan lifted up the piece of paper full of names. "This is a fucking start."

Shit.

It really was the honeypot.

"Send the names to my phone," I said, pulling it from my back pocket.

"No," Lorcan said, standing up and putting the list of names back in the folder.

"What?" Conor asked.

"You just got back. You need sleep, you need to talk to Sloane, and you both look like you need about nine rounds of sex. Go. Ronan won't attack us for a few days at least."

He took the folder with him and left the room. Conor sighed, and leaned back in his chair, running his hands through his hair like he did when he was frustrated.

He wanted this over, just like I did, but I knew Lorcan was right. He was annoyingly always right, in one way or another.

"Go and wake her up," Conor told me. "I bet she can't wait to see you."

"We don't even know what's happening. I swore I'd never pull her down into this cesspit."

"How about you ask her what she wants for once?" Conor answered. "She may surprise you."

He left me standing there, wondering just what the hell I was going to say to Sloane when I went back into that room and woke her up.

How did you say sorry you got caught up in this when you tried to get away from me?

SLOANE

I felt something on my arm, and my senses sparked to life as I gasped, trying to get away. Strong arms held onto me. My eyes finally adjusted to the dark and I saw those familiar eyes I had daydreamed about.

Instantly, I felt relief and I melted into his arms. He held me tight, as he gripped the sides of my face in his hands. Our lips met with ferocity, and I felt his warmth as he kissed me like he never wanted me to go. Feeling his tongue on mine, wrestling for dominance, had sparks shooting down my spine and directly to my pussy. I moaned into his mouth as he pulled me onto his lap. I straddled him, running my hands through his hair, and pulling. Killian growled as he moved his hands up and down my bare thighs, digging his fingers into my skin. His lips moved down my neck, as I began to writhe on top of his lap. His fingers dipped into the elastic of my underwear and he yanked. I could hear the ripping of the fine cotton as he freed my pussy from the material. His own pants were pushed down, our lips never parting during the act. He positioned me over his cock, and I slid down on it. I was wet already, simply from his kiss, but I shouldn't have been surprised. It didn't take much for me to get wet for him. His cock stretched me in the most exciting way ever as I started to move up and down on his cock. It wouldn't take long until I tumbled over the edge. The events of the last couple of weeks had me on edge, but now, I knew I wanted Killian forever. I needed him, no matter how fucking dark he was, I needed him.

All of him.

His hands gripped my hips, digging his nails into my skin, eliciting a delicious pain up and down my sides. I slowed my bouncing so that I could grab one hand and place it over my neck.

He got the picture without further prodding and he squeezed my neck as he sucked my tongue into his mouth. My pussy was throbbing around his cock, as I struggled to breathe with his hand squeezing my throat.

I loved the danger of it.

I loved how he made me feel like I wouldn't be able to breathe until I came over his cock. I lived for him, and him only.

My pussy exploded around his cock as I gripped his shoulders and dug my nails in. He didn't stop clutching at my throat until my spasms had eased. When I collapsed against his shoulder, he removed his hand from my throat and he shoved me onto my back. With a quick movement, he pulled my legs apart, lifting one leg over his shoulder and shoving one thigh to the side of him, he pushed into me again, achingly slow.

"Fuck me," I ground out with a tone I'd never heard from myself before. Killian wasted no time in doing just that. He slammed his cock into me, his balls slapping against me as he fucked his way to his own explosion.

He fucked me in a way that told me just how scared he had been, in a way that proved no man would ever meet up to his standard. I was ruined.

I was his.

Tears slid down my cheeks, and I was thankful in that moment for the dark room as I had Killian fuck me sense-less, just like we both needed after such an ordeal.

He was my home.

My sanctuary.

I needn't be scared of who he was, and I think I always knew that, it was pure fear that had led me to walk away from him.

Fear I somehow no longer had.

———

"WE SHOULD PROBABLY HAVE STARTED with talking," he said once our breathing began to go back to normal. I chuckled, and turned my head to look at him. I looked down at his naked body and it made me want to jump on top of him again and ride him until I collapsed. I never knew I needed him so much before.

"What did you want to talk about?" I asked him.

"Tell me what happened to you."

"I don't want to tell you that, Killian," I replied. "I want to forget it."

"I doubt you will," he said. "Being tortured is hard to forget."

He was right. Every time I closed my eyes, I could see it again, Sinead's crazy eyes, and the way I could predict when she was going to wail on me.

"There was one thing I realized being tied up," I said, sitting up. He sat up as well, but kept his distance, keeping his eyes on me. "That I had been stupid. In the time of thinking I was going to die, several times, all I wanted was to have you march through those doors and shoot every last one of them. I wanted you to save me, I wanted to have the chance to tell you that I should have chosen you all those years ago."

Killian's body tensed and I was worried he would take off, avoid the emotions bubbling to the surface but he needed to hear it. I needed him to hear it.

And I was eagerly awaiting any kind of response from him. He could reject me now, tell me he was never going to settle down and I knew that would be my fault. I broke his heart all those years ago, I had no right to have him open up for me again, but there was a vague hope that maybe he would choose me.

"You know, there have been so many times I wanted to hear you say that you wanted me. I never expected to feel fear when you said to me."

"Fear?"

"Just knowing me has put you in danger, several times now, how could you possibly want this for yourself? You broke up with me because of this shit."

"You don't want me?"

The rejection was hitting home and hard. I wanted to wrap myself up in the sheets and hide under them. But there was also the part of me that wanted to fight for him. He stood up and put his hands on his hips. His cock was lying in between his legs, and it was inviting enough for my eyes to travel down to it again.

"You keep looking at it like that, Sloane, and I'll tie you to the bed and fuck you senseless."

I felt my teeth drag my bottom lip in between them at the prospect of it.

"Sloane..."

It was meant as a warning but I saw the way his body tensed as my gaze raked up and down his body. I felt like a blood thirsty, sex-starved woman who couldn't stop myself and I was in this moment.

"What's that?" I asked, looking at the section of his chest that I hadn't noticed before. I knew he had the family crest on his chest but there was a section under his pec that I hadn't noticed before.

He looked down and relaxed, as he looked back at me. "It's my tatt."

"Yes, I'm aware, but it's not connected to the family crest part."

"It's a separate tattoo," he told me. "It says Sloane."

I got off the bed and moved over to it, holding his body toward the window so I could see it in the light outside. My name was tattooed on his chest, with my favorite flower entwined through the letters.

"When did you do this?" I asked him, surprised that words had formed. I was still in shock.

"The day we broke up."

"Why?" I asked, my voice breaking.

He shrugged his shoulders but I knew he knew the answer. I wanted to know. I needed to know.

"You should rest," he said. He grabbed his jeans and a shirt and took off before I could form words. I sat back down on the bed, the information swirling around in my brain like a disease.

KILLIAN

Walking away from Sloane had been hard. I hadn't exactly hidden the tattoo but for her to see it, it was different. It did things to me, made me realize that all those years ago she hadn't wanted to tough it out with me.

Things hadn't changed.

In fact, I was deeper than I ever thought I would be so if she wanted to be with me, she had to accept who I was now.

Part of me didn't want her to be sullied with the darkness inside of me, and the other part, the dominant part, didn't want to watch her go. In some way, I needed her, but I needed her only if she needed me.

This could be the start of something great or the worst heartache I'd ever known. I climbed out onto the roof from our old parents bedroom. None of us had moved into it, and it had been untouched since Finneas died. We had always come out onto the roof outside the window and sat out here when we needed to get away. Somehow, it cleared my mind and made decisions easier. It had to do with something about the air being clearer up here.

I moved my head to the side when I heard Sloane coming through the window. She came to sit beside me on the roof, just like we had done so many times before.

"Why did it upset you for me to see it?" she asked me. It was a valid question, and one I should know the answer to.

"I don't know."

"Why did you get it?"

"Because I had to say goodbye to you and I needed something to make me feel okay with that," I told her.

"But it's my name. Women wouldn't like that, right?"

"I never cared what women thought of me or my body," I told her. "Only you."

"What's bothering you, Killian? I know it's not me."

"It's not entirely you," I said. "I just...there's things I need to do and I don't think you'll approve."

"What is it?"

"What did you know about my dad?"

"Finneas?" she said. "I knew he was scary. You protected me from him."

"He was also feared."

"Yeah, I remember that. No one spoke about him for fear he would find out."

"And nothing like what is happening to us now ever happened to him."

"You think it has something to do with the way you run things?" she asked me.

I nodded.

"Look, if it were just you or even just Lorcan running things, maybe, but with all three of you...I doubt you could have foreseen what would happen. Ronan is a dick, and he always had been."

"Sloane, as much as I want you to stay here, be with me. There are things that I am going to have to do that you probably won't agree with."

She sighed. "I'm not the same girl I was back when I was head over heels for you. I've been through real shit now. I'm not as sweet as I once was."

"I'm going to take us back to the way Finneas ran things. That means, for a little while, we'll have even more people come for us."

"Are you going after Ronan?"

I nodded. "Yes, all of us are. Teeghan will need to stay here and make sure things run smoothly. When Ronan is taken down, we need to send a message to others who think they can hurt us."

It was a lot to take in. I knew that but we needed to keep our family's legacy intact.

"What are you not telling me, Killian?" she asked.

Fuck, I both loved and hated that she was so intuitive. No one could usually tell what I was thinking.

"You have to know what I do for a living, what I do for this family..."

"I do."

"And you're okay with it?"

She shrugged. "Not totally okay but I'm starting to realize I'm not totally not okay with it either."

"Sloane, I'm going to need to be darker, more reckless," I told her. "I need you to really think about that and decide if that's a life you can live with and if it's not, I will set you up somewhere, maybe overseas, where they can't find you."

I could see the wheels turning in her head, the decision wasn't a light one, and I knew that. My phone dinged, and I saw Conor's name pop up on my screen.

"Conor needs me," I told her. "But take a few days, think about everything. I promise, I will be okay with whatever you choose."

I leant over and kissed her forehead before I found the willpower to walk back to the window and slide through it, heading down the hall before I changed my mind.

The ball was in her court now.

Where it should have been, this entire time.

CHAPTER FOURTEEN

SLOANE

Teeghan was quiet, as we sat at the cafe, sipping her latte. I could see she was going to make me do the talking, at least be the first one to speak.

"Glad to have Conor back?" I asked, hoping to stall. Teeghan was too smart for that, and I could see it in the way she stayed silent. "Fine, Killian gave me an out."

"And?"

"And I don't know why he did that," I admitted. "I'm a little hurt that he doesn't want to fight for me."

Teeghan finally put her mug down on the table and leaned forward. "Sloane, it's not that he doesn't want to fight for you. He dropped everything to go and find you, and I know he always will, I think he's trying to protect you. After all, you didn't want a part of this life for years. It's up to you to choose him, which means choosing this life, or choosing freedom."

"I don't want freedom," I said quickly and to my surprise, I meant it. "I want...him. I think I always have."

Teeghan nodded. "I know, but choosing Killian comes with a price, just like me choosing Conor. My father was killed because I fell in love with him. I had to deal with that on top of loving someone I clearly shouldn't. Instead of blaming him, because we both know it wasn't his fault it happened, I chose to stand beside him, and help him get rid of those who tried to mess with the family."

"You chose Conor."

"I did, and I don't regret it one bit."

"Doesn't it scare you?" I asked her. "Them going off and facing off with these assholes."

"Of course, I'd be a fool if I didn't think when I said goodbye to him, it may be the last time but even if we didn't fall in love with them, and we fell for normal guys. How do we know when we kiss them goodbye, that won't be the last time?"

She was right.

"That's true," I said, leaning back in my chair. "I mean, I never thought that day would be the last time I saw Sean. One freak accident later, and he's gone."

Teeghan frowned but tried to hide it behind her latte.

"What?"

"Sean didn't die in a freak accident, Sloane. He died in a car accident after he was being chased by loan sharks."

I felt as if my mind was about to implode.

"What?"

"Everyone was lied to, but a few months ago, I found out the truth. Sean had gotten into some serious debt and he needed an out. Instead of going to the O'Farrell's, who could have easily helped him, he got in deeper and deeper."

"Wait...Tee...this doesn't make sense. If he had debt, it would have passed to me, and I got nothing."

"Because it was paid before you found out," Teeghan said. "Look, Sean hated Killian, and he had every right to because he knew you were still in love with him. Killian chose to stay away, because he knew seeing you happy with someone else would kill him inside but he would have helped Sean in a heartbeat if it meant keeping you happy. Sean was just too proud to ask for help from him and it got him killed."

My mind was rushing about, trying to process the news that the caring and loving husband I thought had been an angel had been addicted to gambling to the point he'd been killed for it.

"Killian never said a word to me."

"He knew you needed time."

"I feel like I'm betraying Sean," I said, finally. "Killian was someone he hated."

"But you never hated him," Teeghan said. "Sean was my brother and I loved the fucker but you need to say goodbye or you'll never be happy."

I nodded, knowing she was right.

She finished her drink and stood. "I have to go anyway. Go and say goodbye to what's been holding you back all these years. Then decide."

"But what if he decides in a few months time that I'm not enough?" I asked her, before I stood. "What if in a few months, he's visiting other womens' beds all night?"

Teeghan put her sunglasses on and smirked at me. "Sloane, that man has been obsessed with you since the first day he saw you. Take a leap of faith and believe you are enough."

She pulled me into a hug and said her goodbyes before she headed off to her car. I got in my own car and started to drive. At first, I didn't know where to go and drove around aimlessly until I turned onto the motorway and headed toward Galway.

When I pulled up outside the cemetery, I knew that my heart and my brain were finally working in unison.

I got out and headed toward Sean's grave. It was relatively fresh compared to the battered and age worn headstones on either side of his. A reminder that it hadn't been so long ago I had been a married woman, living an honest life.

Apparently, a life full of secrets.

"Teeghan told me how you died earlier," I said to the headstone even though I knew it was useless. "I wish you had told me, but then again, you always were too proud to admit you needed help. God, you know, I loved you. I loved you so much, Sean. You were exactly what I needed after Killian but it pains me to say that I knew you knew. I knew you were aware I couldn't stop loving Killian and I'm sorry that you knew that."

Tears rolled down my cheeks as I put my hand on the top of his headstone.

"I tried, Sean. I really did, but I've waited years to move on out of respect for you because of that love and probably the guilt that came along with it. I have to stop feeling guilty because it's eating me up inside."

God, Sloane, you've really gone and lost it now, haven't you? Talking to a fucking headstone like he's still there.

I stood up, wiped the tears away from my face and looked down at his name etched into the marble.

"Goodbye, Sean."

KILLIAN

Conor was grating on my nerves with his leg moving up and down anxiously. It was like his leg had a life of its own. Lorcan read through the paperwork in front of him, his two close advisors behind him, waiting for instruction. I didn't like to wait, and this was going to do my head in if he didn't fucking speak and soon.

The doors opened and I saw Teeghan breeze in as if she had just come from a luxury spa. How the hell was that woman so deep in our family already and still looked as if nothing had cracked her yet?

She smiled at us all before she headed down toward the kitchen. Conor's spirit lifted and his inane anxious leg bounce was gone. It was amazing how one little person could calm that fucking guy down. He was a loose cannon before her, and now I didn't even know what to call the fucker.

It made me think of Sloane.

Just being in her presence had a calm settle over me like I couldn't believe. The relief I'd felt when I'd seen her asleep in my bed, and the way she relaxed when she realized it was me waking her had my cock doing all sorts of shit under my pants.

I willed the thought of Sloane out of my mind so I could focus on the task at hand and get out of here.

Lorcan's men finally moved out of the room and he focused on us again.

"Turns out Ronan fled the country after Sinead and Darren were killed. Seems we have a little while before he comes for us again."

"We can't just give up," I aimed at him. "Come on, look what he's fucking done because we didn't go after him when we should have."

"Sit down, Killian."

187

I hadn't realized I'd gotten up until he'd said that. I calmly sat down and tried to focus my attention on not losing my shit.

"There's something else we should be worried about."

Conor and I both stared at our older brother, on the edge of our seats. What could be fucking that bad that we needed to worry more?

"Well?" I asked, impatiently.

He shoved a photo over to me. I grabbed it from the table and looked at it, shock filtering through my body as I looked down at the CCTV image of Ronan with a familiar looking woman.

"Amity."

"Looks like Ronan and Amity are working together," Lorcan said.

"Fuck," I shoved the photo away from me and sat back in my chair. How the fuck could this happen?

"Where did they go?" Conor asked.

"Outside of Europe. We can't touch him but I do have an alert on him. The second he returns to either England or Ireland, we'll nab him."

"And if he never returns?" Conor asked.

"He will," I said. "He wants Ireland. Let him come and fucking try to take it off us."

Lorcan nodded. "I have to go, I'll see you all tomorrow. Killian, you may want to check on your businesses since you've been gone for so long."

Lorcan left the estate and I turned to Conor for an explanation. Since when did Lorcan leave?

"Oh, you didn't know?" Conor asked, standing up and chuckling. "Big bro has taken up with one of the whores he looks after."

"From Sassy's?"

"Either that or the Station X studios."

When Lorcan took over the brothels, gentlemen clubs and the porn industry in Ireland, we'd all thought he would close them down. He wasn't someone who openly flaunted his sex life, if he even had one, but instead, he'd turned them into steady streams of income for the family.

"That's not like him."

"It's about time he got some," Conor said. "Now, if you'll excuse me. I'll be with Tee."

I nodded as he walked out of the room and left me alone. Lorcan was right. I'd left the businesses with my men to look after while I was gone. It was long past due that I visited and checked on them before they went to shit.

Amity and Ronan were going to have to wait.

———

THE MUSIC PUMPED hard as I looked out over the dancers below me. It was nice and quiet up on my balcony, and the club was still doing very well. It was still one of the most profitable businesses in our family. My mind hadn't stopped thinking about Sloane and what she could potentially say.

I know I had left it up to her, but I was nervous she would walk away and I would have to move on without her. Obviously, I wouldn't blame her for that decision but I couldn't imagine not having those eyes looking into mine.

If she chose to walk away, I would die alone. There would never be another like her.

I slapped myself across the face to push the shit in my brain to get out. This was not Killian O'Farrell. The man people feared when I walked into a room. This was something Conor would be saying to himself.

Suddenly, I felt like I wasn't alone on the balcony. I was about to get up when I felt the hands clasp around my neck, fingers running through my hair and pulling my head back. Sloane's eyes met mine as I looked at her from upside down. Her lips were on mine as quick as I could move. I liked this forward Sloane, it was rare for her to come out but when she did. I would do pretty much anything for her.

She pulled away and let go of my neck. "I didn't expect to be able to sneak up on you. You going soft, O'Farrell."

She slid onto my lap, and straddled me, putting her arms around my neck.

"Around you, I'll never be soft."

She leaned in and kissed me softly, a kiss that would lead to so much more.

"I guess you've decided," I said to her.

Her lips dropped to mine again, her tongue pushing into my mouth into a fierce and mind blowing kiss. She broke the kiss finally, so we could catch our breath.

"That clear enough for you?" she asked. I squeezed her butt tight and pushed her up against my rock hard cock under my pants to show her just what a life with me would entail.

Grabbing a handful of hair, I pulled her back in for a kiss.

I was never going to get sick of kissing the hell out of this woman.

She was *mine*.

THE END

OTHER BOOKS BY KATE

The O'Farrell Brothers

Conor

A Woman Scorned

Mine, Forever

Havoc

Standalone Dark Romance

Deny Thy Name

King

Contemporary Romances

Change of Plans

Rise Above